Do No Harm
Mishaps of Misguided Medical Sleuths

*A humorous account of what doctors face on
the clinical battlefield,
fighting against nature, insurance
restrictions, hospital administrators,
and personal limitations, all while
admonished to Do No Harm.*

Part fiction, part memoir

Alice Faryna, M.D.

Dedication

In gratitude to all the people who taught me the practice of medicine: the patients who entrusted their personal stories to me, who put aside their pain and weariness so that I could learn how to do physical examinations, attempt invasive procedures, and lamely try to answer the existential question, "Why did this happen to me?" They understood that the supply of physicians must continually be replenished, so they smiled at my ineptitude, and encouraged me to stay the course.

Acknowledgements

My earlier writings are limited to publications in medical journals or textbooks. A life-long avid reader of all types of books, I tried my hand at writing a few years after retirement. I work better with deadlines, so I joined NaNoWriMo. (National Novel Writing Month is a 501(c)(3) nonprofit that offers an online challenge and support to write 50,000 words in the month of November.) I did not succeed the first time, but hit the magic number in November of 2015. With the encouragement of the local chapter of the International Women Writers Guild, these early fragments coalesced into a novel. I am indebted to the constructive feedback of its members, especially the facilitator, Jeanne Marlowe, and from proofreader Jim Cowan. My daughter, Dana Ashrawi, provided technical support in the final formatting process. My granddaughter, Alice Ashrawi, designed the book cover. My publishing coach, Sandee Hemphill, introduced me to the unfamiliar world of publishing and marketing, keeping me on track to complete this contribution to my bucket list.

Kate

Shortly after 11 PM, Kate finally pulled into her garage. She looked at the caved in trunk, noticing the license plate was mangled so badly that the 2014 registration sticker was invisible. She muttered to herself, "How much will my insurance go up after this . . . even though it wasn't my fault." She picked up the mail and climbed wearily up the porch steps. Opening the door, she stepped into the foyer, threw the mail on the floor, and kicked off her Ferragamo pumps. One flew into the dining room, landing under the table where Buspar was napping. It struck him on the nose. He gave Kate a startled look and then padded over warily, no doubt wondering what he could have done wrong in just a few seconds. She dropped her keys on the kitchen counter, picked up a biscuit from the counter and gave it to him, patting him on the head to reassure him that he was not in trouble.

Turning on the kitchen light, she headed for the furiously blinking answering machine on the corner desk. The first three messages were from the hospital. Mr. Vitko's potassium level was 3.2; the AIDS patient had a temperature of 104; Mrs. Catoni did not have a laxative order and was adamant that something be done that night to get her bowels moving again. Kate called the nurse and informed her that Mr. Vitko had enough potassium in his IV to take care of the problem, that the AIDS patient should have another round of blood cultures but no change in antibiotics, and that Mrs. Catoni could be given a Dulcolax suppository. The nurse then asked what she should do about Mr. Catoni, who brought in tons of fast food for his wife. She was supposed to be on a 1000-calorie diet. Kate choked back the urge to tell her to stick the Dulcolax container up his ass, but managed to deflect the problem to the endocrinologist on the case since it was his job to keep her from lapsing back into hyperosmolar coma, a result of her neglected diabetes.

The fourth message was from her old friend and colleague Anna, who asked her to call back immediately as their vacation plans were in jeopardy. The last message was from a man who wanted to talk to her about her Geo Prism. She was puzzled at first as she no longer had the car, and then remembered that she had given the car to her cleaning lady two years ago. Guessing the caller must be Joyce's deadbeat brother, she deleted the message. Attending Joyce's funeral last week had been quite enough contact with that family.

What she wanted at this point was a glass of wine to soothe her rattled nerves. There was no Chablis left in the refrigerator, but after rummaging around in the cupboard she found a couple of bottles of Two Buck Chuck red wine she had purchased from Trader Joe's a month ago, intending to take it to a potluck which she managed to miss. A search for a corkscrew was, as usual, for naught. She selected two small paring knives, sat down in the doorway and maneuvered the knives on opposite sides of the cork, creating a simulation of the type of wine openers favored by waiters. With her back braced against the door frame and her feet on the opposite frame, she put the bottle between her knees and pushed the knives down to the hilt. Slowly she teased the cork upward. In her zeal, she succeeded only in snapping one of the handles off the knife blade.

By this time the goal was no longer to drink a glass of wine, but to assert her dominion over at least one thing in her life. She found a hammer and a rusty but serviceable metal file at the bottom of the toolbox in the utility room. The file obligingly carved a groove into the neck of the bottle. She sat down at the kitchen table, laid the bottle on its side and raised the hammer to strike off the neck containing the offending cork. Buspar had followed her into the kitchen hoping for more treats. Just as Kate was at maximum downswing with the hammer, Buspar placed his head in her lap, distracting her attention from the bottle. The hammer struck the body of the bottle. Shards of glass flew in all directions and red wine splashed onto her Neiman Marcus jacket. A string of expletives sent Buspar running for the basement. Kate placed her head on the table and moaned. Then she cleared a path through the debris and retrieved Buspar, assuring him he was her one true love and the only thing that kept her going. After finding some cooking sherry in the refrigerator, she dumped it into a tumbler and drained it on her way to the bedroom. She retrieved her cell phone from her soggy jacket and sent a text to her husband, Michael, who was visiting his parents in Seattle. She had already called him about the highway accident, but she wanted him to know that though she was safely home, she was not to be disturbed for the next eight hours. Too tired to attend to her clothes, she discarded her suit and blouse on the floor, pulled off her panty hose and put on one of Michael's oversized T-shirts. With just enough energy left to assemble her CPAP machine, she adjusted the face mask and fell into bed.

She was awakened by a shrill noise in the middle of one

of her frequent frustration dreams in which she tries desperately to get to the airport on time, but cannot find her ticket; then her car is missing, and all the people she calls for help are otherwise occupied or disinterested in her plight. At first she thought it was the siren of an ambulance called to cart her off to a locked ward. Rousing to consciousness, she realized it was her bedside phone ringing. The clock registered 9 AM, so she was already late for her part-time job at a local HMO where she did medical review. Since she didn't play golf, she thought it prudent to use her Wednesdays off to earn some extra money without the grief of dealing with desperately ill or dysfunctional patients. She picked up the phone, and hoping she sounded alert she said, "Sorry I didn't call you. I had a plumbing emergency this morning. I should be there within the hour."

There was a brief silence on the line. Then she heard Anna say, "Does that mean you backed into a fire hydrant or you got home so late Buspar had peed on the sofa?"

"Oh Anna, I swear to God, I really did have an emergency. You won't believe this. After finishing consults at 9 PM, I was heading home on the freeway—"

Anna could sense another one of Kate's marathon stories in the making. She tried to interrupt. "Wait a sec, let's clear up the reservations first."

"Screw the reservations. You've got to hear this. It's friggin' unbelievable. I was just a half mile away from my exit when I saw this red convertible in the rearview mirror coming at me like a rocket. There was a car in every lane and a car 20 feet in front of me. I hit my brakes hoping he would see the lights. He did slam on his brakes but he still ended up in my trunk. I shot across the highway, landing in the median strip facing the opposite direction. And Anna, would you believe it, suddenly all the cars disappeared and there wasn't one in sight for half a mile. No witnesses!"

"Good grief. Were you hurt?"

"No. I got out of my car figuring we had to exchange insurance information. Also to take a photo of my car. The red Mercedes was on the shoulder on the right side. I saw the airbags had deployed and it looked like the left front wheel had major damage. The driver was struggling to get out so at least I wasn't going to have to do CPR. When he finally emerged, I thought, Oh shit, I'm about to be wiped out by a drug lord. The guy was sporting a bushy Afro, black leather pants, a couple of diamond rings, and a half-dozen gold chains around his neck. I held out my card and said very politely, 'I guess we need to exchange some insurance information'. He waved my hand away and said almost graciously, 'Can we handle this privately? I'd rather not involve the insurance companies. What would it cost to repair your trunk and bumper? Doesn't look like there is any other damage.' With that he pulled out a money clip and peeled off 10 $100 bills."

"Well that sounds right friendly!" laughed Anna.

"Thankfully. I did a quick calculation. My deductible is at least $500 and I knew the repair estimate would be lower if I told them insurance was not available. At the same time, who knows if the money is real? Buying some time, I said, 'Looks like you are going to need a tow truck.' He agreed, but there was a bigger problem. The car belongs to his wife and he would just as soon she didn't hear details about this accident."

Kate paused to quickly check her cell phone for urgent texts. There being none, she continued. "Seems this guy is a coach for some football team in the minor leagues. Forgot the name . . . likely some slimy animal. The way he drives they should be called the Rams! He was on his way to a sports convention in Atlanta and had stopped to visit a friend in Knoxville, which of course is not on the route from Jacksonville where he lives, to Atlanta. It doesn't take a genius to figure out his friend is not someone his wife would approve of."

Anna by now was resigned to hearing the unedited story, which was turning out to be rather entertaining after all. She said. "I imagine it will take him some time to fabricate a story about the smashed Mercedes."

Kate continued, "That's his problem. Pretty soon we saw the flashers of a patrol car heading for us. Someone must've called in a 911. Well, the police officer of course wanted name, rank, and serial number as recorded on our licenses. The coach pulled his wallet out and handed over his license. I gave the officer my registration papers, which were in the glove compartment, and said I would be glad to give him my license if he could pry open my trunk where I keep my purse when I'm in the hospital. That turned out to be impossible so he decided to focus on the rammer, to whom he issued a ticket for reckless driving, and did a Breathalyzer test, which he passed. He told me I could go home, but warned that I would have to come in for a written testimony later in the week. The officer called the towing company and drove off. There being no witnesses now, I was glad to accept the offer of a grand and we parted the best of friends. He even offered to send me two tickets to the next game in Atlanta."

Anna ventured a change of topic. "Kate if you could handle another decision today I'd like to finalize reservations for our upcoming vacation."

"I thought you had reservations for someplace in Hocking Hills."

"Reservations for Glenlaurel were sold out for the next two months, so I made one for the Spa at Cedar Falls, but it is a week later.

"Let me check my calendar . . . O.K. go ahead and reserve it. My car should be repaired by then."

There was a brief silence as neither woman could think of what to say next. Anna spoke first.

"Kate, how do you do it?" she asked.

Kate bristled. "Name one thing I could've done yesterday that would have changed anything. And speaking of yesterday, did I tell you my cleaning lady died? The funeral was something else . . ."

Anna interrupted. "Hold on. Tell me about it on the way to Cedar Falls. I'm not sure I can take any more drama. And say hi to Michael for me."

"Will do, as soon as he gets back from visiting his parents. He thinks they are going to need assisted living pretty soon and they are resisting the notion. Christ, look at the time. I'd better get my car to the dent place and find a way to get to work."

Anna

Anna returned the phone to its cradle while exhaling a sigh of relief. She leaned back in the recliner chair recalling her many adventures with Kate. They had met over 30 years ago as new faculty members of the fledgling medical school in Dayton, Ohio. Anna, the elder by 12 years, was dealing with a marriage in its death throes. Kate had just finished her specialty training in infectious diseases and was eagerly looking forward to her first job that paid a living wage. As they tried to build a social life, a challenge for single professional women, they quickly became close friends. Anna, who was adapting to life as a single mom with two teenaged children, was cautious, methodical and often worried about financial security. She was respected as a good clinician by the rest of the faculty. A tall, slender brunette, active in a variety of sports, she especially liked to ski and play golf. She had married a medical school classmate, who was initially a good husband and father to their children, but never satisfied with a variety of jobs in the medical profession. The marriage ended after a number of disrupting moves around the country followed by his decision to abandon medicine and pursue a new career in the theater.

Kate's over-sized body on a 5-foot 10-inch frame presented an intimidating presence to the men she met, both professionally and socially. In addition, she had an assertive manner, which, combined with her zero tolerance for fools, did not endear her to some of the other faculty members. At their age, the number of suitable men for dating was very limited. Time after time, following a particularly disappointing outing, Kate would say to Anna, "Time to start turning over the rocks again and see what crawls out this time."

"Have you ever noticed," Anna would reply, "that often the nicest guys are married to perfectly dreadful women?"

"That does seem to be a pattern. Maybe we are being too nice."

Over the next several years Anna and Kate created a social life built around interest groups and clubs that they enjoyed. The Sierra Club was their favorite venue for trips. In addition, they traveled together to medical conventions and Kate would often be invited to join Anna when she and her two children went to Florida to visit family. It was during these trips that Kate developed a reputation for inviting dramatic and unexpected sideshows. The kids nicknamed her "Mame" after the flamboyant character created by Patrick Dennis in the 1955 novel *Auntie Mame*.

Eventually Kate got tired of academic medicine and the cold northern winters. She moved to Florida where she established a solo practice in infectious diseases. While living there, Kate was briefly married to a bipolar man whose financial escapades during his manic phases eventually led her to divorce him. She fled to Tennessee and at the tender age of 40 married a sane man who taught high school biology and was heavily involved in a variety of liberal causes. Kate fondly referred to him as 'My Cadillac-communist sweetie.' His most lovable attribute was that he was a good cook and happily took over that part of the housekeeping. Anna never remarried. Their friendship continued, as did occasional vacations together. Anna, now retired, with more time to indulge hobbies and travel, looked forward to some quality time with her friend.

She turned to her inevitable "to-do" list, one of several she had planted in various rooms in the house, and worked out a route for errands to do in the morning. The evening would be occupied by a meeting of the Social Justice committee at her church. She was due to make a report on her favorite project: Single Payer Health Care. Anna was on the executive committee of this statewide group whose mission was to expand Medicare to all Ohioans. The state legislature was equally determined to have nothing to do with big government programs.

Her commitment to this activity grew out of her last job. Fifteen years earlier she had left her academic position in Dayton to become the first medical director for the Medicare part B program in Ohio and West Virginia. Like most physicians, she was not aware of how the medical insurance system in the United States worked. But she was acutely aware that it began to change drastically in the 1980s. As an academic physician, she also had a small private practice within the University. At first it was fun. Then she found herself called upon by people representing HMOs and PPOs asking her to become one of their preferred providers for a smaller but guaranteed fee schedule. Another source of irritation was the hospital, which had hired an army of administrators committed to increase its profits. One of them called her in one day and pointed out that the outpatient clinics (she supervised one for the Department of Internal Medicine) were not making any money. His manner was definitely accusatory. Of course they weren't making money. Most of the clinic patients were indigent. The most maddening part of the evolving system was that sometimes her private paying patients would disappear without warning. Presumably they were being seen by some other physicians, but she never got a request for a summary of their records. Occasionally the lost patients would reappear, informing her that when she had been dropped from their preferred provider list, they were forced to change physicians. A few years later, she was once again on the preferred provider list of the insurance company currently used by their employers, so they returned to her practice. It seems no one in insurance companies gave a hoot for the benefits of continuity in care.

When an opportunity to apply her medical skills in a totally different way was offered to her, she quickly accepted a job with the Medicare program. She found, much to her surprise, that sometimes big government programs work very well. Furthermore, the Medicare population of patients had much more financial security than people who were not yet 65. Although their retirement incomes were smaller than before, they no longer faced catastrophic medical costs. After 10 years of administrative medicine, she retired from the Medicare job, and eagerly embraced a small but dedicated group of activists who thought the United States should do what every other capitalist country had done years, if not decades, earlier: provide universal healthcare. And in her view, that meant Medicare for everyone.

The upcoming vacation was scheduled to begin in May. Naturally, Anna had to prepare another to-do list centering on the trip. First, get a tour book from AAA on Ohio, check the weather reports, then arrange for someone to come in a couple of times during her week away to take care of her Burmese cat, Sumei. As she was jotting down these thoughts, the cat in question jumped up on the desk and started nibbling on the free edge of her notepad. She scratched him under the chin saying "I'm going to desert you again in a couple of weeks, but Joan will come in and play with you." Then she placed him on the floor, picked up her purse and left to start her errands.

On Vacation

On an unseasonably warm May evening, Kate pulled into Anna's driveway. By the time she had retrieved her overnight bag and stepped out of the car, Anna was running down the front steps to greet her.

"Oh Kate, it is so good to see you again!"

"It is so good to not be in Tennessee right now," she replied giving Anna a warm hug. "How about I just leave my car in the driveway? I'd be happy to drive since my car is larger than yours and who knows what kind of artworks we will bring back from the local artisans."

"Fine with me. Have you had dinner yet?"

"Just snacks. I brought a bottle of your favorite Riesling. Have you prepared something that will go with it?"

"Everything goes with Riesling. I wasn't sure when you would you get here, so I'm planning on grilled salmon and asparagus. No dessert. We'll come back 10 pounds heavier anyway."

Upon entering the house, Kate took her overnight bags into the guest room and was joined by Sumei, who leapt on the bed to examine the contents of the bag that held her CPAP machine.

"You stay on the floor my friend," said Kate as she whisked him off the bed. "But you can't sleep here. I'm allergic to you."

Meanwhile, Anna had put the salmon under the broiler and the asparagus in the microwave. She placed some freshly baked rolls on the table along with a bowl of fruit salad. As she poured the wine into goblets, Kate appeared, sat down and picked up the tour book. She sipped her wine as she leafed through pages about Hocking Hills. "It looks like there are some nice hiking trails around here."

"Yes, there are lots of lovely places to walk through. Old Man's Cave is especially popular." Anna checked the salmon, and concluding that it was flaky enough to eat, she removed it from the oven, placing it on a gilded Christmas platter, which she used regularly because it always ended up at the top of the stack of platters and she had never gotten around to putting the platter back with the Christmas collection. She brought the salmon along with a small bowl of dill sauce to the table. After draining the asparagus and sprinkling it with Parmesan cheese, she placed it on the table and called Kate to join her.

"I never got a follow-up on your car accident. Did the illicit thousand dollars cover the damages?

"Not quite, but since my deductible was $1000, I figure the extra $500 I had to pay was worth not using the insurance."

During dinner, Kate and Anna spent two hours reminiscing about past adventures, trips, catching up on family, and a detailed account of Michael's latest project to save the world from itself. They retired a little after 10 o'clock, agreeing to get up at 6 AM and be on the road by 7 AM. They actually managed to be in the car and backing out of the driveway by 7:30. Soon they were on the freeway heading south for Route 33.

Kate exhaled a deep sigh. "I have a big announcement to make. Didn't want to get into it last night. I decided to close my practice and have accepted an offer from TennHealth to oversee their medical review for Medicare and Medicaid."

"Wow," said Anna. "That's a pretty big decision. Seems pretty sudden, unless you've been holding out on me."

"Kind of sudden, but I used to envy you somewhat when you worked for Medicare. You seemed to be having so much fun most of the time. And you didn't have to be on call at night anymore."

"It was kind of fun—especially the fraud investigations. Some of the crooks were remarkably creative. I wish now I had kept a diary. It would make quite a book."

"I could write a book too. But I would probably be sued for libel, so I can't do it until everybody else is dead."

"Was there something that triggered the decision, or was the offer from TennHealth too tempting?"

"Well lean back and listen because this is a long story. I had been feeling burned out for about a year. Then Michael and I would go on a vacation and I would recover. But I never recovered 100%. The last straw, or tipping point you might say, happened when I was making rounds a couple of days after the accident. I had been asked to consult on a charming young man who had a severe opportunistic infection related to AIDS. His white count was dangerously low and even though his infection was treatable—it was pneumonia from pneumocystis carinii— and I was worried. He was not responding well, running high fevers, chills and sweats. The case was complicated because he had also developed lymphoma. However the antiviral drugs seemed to be working because the viral load was going down, so I was hopeful that he might make it. As optimistic as you can be for complicated cases. Then I called some folks at the NIH and discussed the case with one of their experts.

"Had they ever seen that particular situation?"

"Yes, quite a few. They said we could either treat the AIDS and he would die of lymphoma, or treat the lymphoma and he would die of AIDS. Pick the poison of your choice."

"I don't think I could ever handle your specialty," Anna mused. "Rheumatology was bad enough. Often well described as the diagnosis and treatment of incurable diseases. But it wasn't all that common for my patients to be critically ill."

"While I was examining him," continued Kate, "in comes this oncologist who's supposed to be treating the lymphoma. A camel jockey from Iran I think."

Anna chuckled. "Now, now. Isn't that a bit racist?"

"I meant that as an epithet specifically for him, not all mid-Easterners. I had run into him before and found him to be remarkably shallow. Orders every lab test in the book instead of examining people. Sometimes he would be confronted by a colleague about an over-zealous treatment plan, and his standard answer was, 'But he has insurance!' On this particular day he exceeded my lowest expectations. While I was writing a note in the record, I overheard him say to the patient that the treatment he proposed would require a bone marrow transplant. Then, now get this Anna, then he says with a perfectly straight face, 'You are still a young man. You might wish to have children someday. We should obtain a sample of your semen and freeze it so that you can use it later on. You must do this now because for the bone marrow transplant we will have to give you radiation and chemotherapy which could damage your sperm'."

"Good grief," exclaimed Anna. "He wants to freeze

semen that's loaded with the AIDS virus for future use?"

"You got it. I was just about to break all rules of professional ethics and tell the lad to throw this charlatan out. I wasn't sure that he was coherent enough to even understand what the man was saying. But he was. He's lying there like a wilted piece of lettuce, staring at the ceiling and mumbling replies to my questions in a faint voice. Then, when he heard the proposal from the oncologist, this wilted piece of lettuce sat up, stared at the man and said, 'That's the stupidest god damn thing I've ever heard.' Then he fell back on his pillow and refused to say anything more. I left the room immediately so I could laugh in private."

Anna sighed. "Makes you wonder how people like that manage to get licensed."

"Oh, his IQ is just fine. It's the way he uses his knowledge that is the problem. It comes back to money," replied Kate. "Some doctors are in cahoots with hospital management to order as many services and tests as possible. Maybe in return for admitting privileges. Who knows? And of course, freezing semen for future use is a legitimate option for some patients but not those who are HIV-positive."

"So this was the tipping point for you?"

"Indeed it was. I was getting increasingly dissatisfied with private practice for over a year. I resented being told by bean counters how to practice medicine. Then I had to hire two billing clerks to handle claims for 12 different insurers. Then each insurance company insisted that I update my credentials every two years for each one separately. Why doesn't someone just create a database that everyone can access?"

"So have you actually closed your practice?"

"I gave myself twenty-four hours to see if this was a temporary meltdown. It wasn't. I woke up the next morning feeling joyful at the prospect of getting out of the snake pit."

"Wow. How's it going?"

"First I notified my staff to take no more appointments or consults and that they should start looking for another job as theirs would end in a couple of months. They have been sending out letters to my regular patients telling them I would forward their records to anyone they chose, giving them some suggestions of good Infectious Diseases specialists. The final step was to resign from the hospitals where I have privileges."

"How did Michael take this news?"

"It turns out he was way ahead of me. Of course he has been listening to me whining and griping about the downward spiral of medical care. He anticipated that I would throw in the towel eventually but didn't say anything to me. He was posting stuff on his Facebook page when I told him I was going to quit private practice. He just looked up from the computer and said, 'I didn't think you would last this long. Congratulations.' What a relief that was."

"So what's next?"

"Well, as I told you before, I had been approached by TennHealth a few times to consider going full time. So I went in for some interviews and negotiated a position where I will be supervising the work of other part-time physicians doing medical review. I told them I couldn't start full time until I got back from vacation."

"Congratulations. What's your reading on the administrative climate at TennHealth? I remember some of my counterparts found it difficult to work with the particular private insurance company that did claims processing for Medicare."

"My immediate supervisor is great. He has clued me in on the hierarchy and warned me about which ones to be wary of. He has chronic kidney disease which is likely to lead to dialysis or a transplant sometime in the near future. Told me he wants someone to groom as his replacement and views me as the best candidate."

"That sounds like the perfect job."

"Yes. I don't want to be stuck in just reviewing claims for the next ten years. I think I have the skills to help develop coverage policy and best practices, so having a mentor pave the way for me is a sweetheart deal."

"We're getting close to our exit. Watch for the one to Logan. And I have something new to tell you also. I've been thinking of doing something special for my 70th birthday this year."

"That's in September, right?" queried Kate.

"Yes, it's on September second."

"Something special, hmmm? You've already tried skiing and ballroom dancing. How about something exciting like a motorcycle trip to the West Coast?"

"That's not exciting—that's suicidal. What came to mind last night as we were reminiscing, was that it would be fun to throw a birthday party and invite the friends we made when we were on the faculty at Wright State. I would pay for one night's lodging at a local motel if they'd be willing to make the trip. Some are still in Dayton, and others, like you, have moved away from Dayton, so it could be a big trip for them."

"How many were you thinking of inviting?"

"Well, including spouses, about 25 to 30. Judging from past experience with hosting parties, only about half of the invitees actually show up. So it should be about 15. Of course that doesn't include you and Michael, but you would be staying in my house."

"Well, count me in. I am sure Michael will want to do the cooking and I will spring for the booze."

"Offers accepted. Assuming Michael agrees."

"He will. Any ideas for entertainment?"

"Yes. Remember the time you and I threw a party at my home in Kettering and sent the guests on a treasure hunt? It was hilarious. I'd love to repeat that."

"Really? At that party all the guests had lived in the area for years and knew the city. How can they do that in unfamiliar territory?"

"Of course it would take some careful planning, including maps with good landmarks. But I think it is doable. These days everyone has a cell phone and a GPS so driving in a strange city wouldn't be all that difficult."

Kate reached for a mini cheesecake she had placed in her tote bag. "That may work. Let's think about it over the next few days. Is this the exit to Logan? Where are we staying?"

"Yes, take route 664. I've been at the Spa at Cedar Falls before so I'll navigate."

Party Plans

The two friends checked into a room at the Inn and then treated themselves to a relaxing massage at the Spa. At a sumptuous dinner that evening, they looked over the area attractions. Amused to find a museum devoted to collectible washboards, they decided instead to plan a trip to a nearby glass museum, and on the next day a hike at Rockbridge State Natural Preserve. Old Man's Cave would be a stop on the last day on the way back to Columbus.

Over lunch the next day they resumed a lengthy discussion about which colleagues to invite to the upcoming birthday party. "I'd really like to see some of my friends from the infectious diseases division," began Kate while digging in to her fish and chips basket. "How about Rob Wheeler and Jules Filstein? Or maybe Dominic Cinzano?"

"It would be a hoot if Chuck Novak could come," replied Anna as she attacked a large Caesar salad. "He has a great sense of humor and is an excellent pianist as well. Maybe he would do some music for us. I'd also like to see George McGee. He is a philosopher, not a physician but he did a great job teaching medical ethics to the medical students."

Kate continued. "Another one who is a hoot is Beth Fowler. She and her husband Roger Comfort developed a joint practice in couples counseling after they got married. And wouldn't you know, they ended up getting divorced themselves."

"I hadn't heard about the divorce. Are you sure? I like them both, and invited them to all of my parties. Do we just invite both of them and see how that falls out?"

"I'm quite sure that they have split. I get regular holiday cards from George and Debbie McGee, and they mentioned it a couple of years ago. I would go ahead and invite both of them."

"I think I'll invite Sheilah and Eric Conrad also. They were in the Family Practice Department, not Internal Medicine. But we socialized regularly. And what about Pat Soffit? She was one of the more amiable people in the Surgery Department. Did you know she kept putting off getting her hepatitis B immunization after it was recommended for all physicians likely to be exposed to that virus? And then she developed jaundice one day. Sure enough it was hep B!"

"Well you know the old adage. He who treats himself has a fool for a physician." Kate now turned her attention to a large serving of bread pudding. "What's the story on Pat? I heard rumors that her husband is gay. Are they still married?"

"Indeed they are. And apparently are a very happy and committed couple. It's an interesting story. As you may know, they were married when she lived in California. Her schedule as a surgeon was very hectic, so she had hired Ted to take care of the grounds and maintenance of the house. He is actually an insurance agent, but did odd jobs when the business was slack. Eventually he also took over the cooking and helped keep the bills somewhat organized. In a few years he had become an essential part of her life. She didn't want her assets to go to her dysfunctional family so they got married. When they moved to Dayton, no one knew what the situation was. I was her personal physician when she got hepatitis, so that's how I learned about it. It has been an enduring marriage. Apparently no romance and she never had kids, so there was little to fight over."

"Yes, the big three marriage busters are money, kids and sex. Seems they only have money to squabble about, and she has plenty of that," observed Kate. "Who was the pulmonary specialist who never could quit smoking? Ben somebody. And how about Carlos, the refugee from Nicaragua who had to take his neurology training all over again because our Boards don't recognize training in other countries?"

"Carlos would be a wonderful addition. And a party is not complete without Harvey Schulman. Besides, given the average age of this crowd, it would be nice to have a cardiologist who can do CPR competently. Also Jean Chang. She took over the combined pediatric/general internal medicine residency after I left, and I hear she did a great job. We used to go on ski trips together."

"Don't forget Dave Brunk. He is another party animal."

"Especially charming to the ladies. How many times has he been married?"

"Lost count. You'd think he would just settle for polyamory instead of serial polygamy. Think of all that alimony."

"Well, rumor has it that he comes from a family with big money. All the kids have trusts so he doesn't need to work to pay the bills."

Anna continued jotting down notes as they chatted about the faculty members fondly remembered. "I'm going to call the alumni office after we get back and try to get updated emails and home addresses. It's getting close to June. The invitations need to be sent by the middle of the month. A lot of people will already have made their summer plans so maybe the list of those sending regrets will be more than 50%."

"I will leave that in your capable hands," declared Kate. "Let's go on that hike at the Nature Preserve now."

The Cleaning Lady's Funeral

The next day they relaxed in a hot tub after breakfast to relieve sore muscles. In the afternoon they drove around the area stopping at craft shops and independent artisans where they purchased some local paintings and crafts. The evening was spent packing, and on the following morning they drove to Old Man's Cave to take pictures. Then Kate found her way back to Route 33 and they were soon heading back to Columbus.

"Did I ever finish telling you what happened the day before the accident?" asked Kate.

"No, I cut you off so we could finish making the reservations for this trip. All I remember is you said something about a funeral. Had you assassinated someone in your favorite insurance company for denying one of your consults?"

"Only in my fantasies. I had this wonderful cleaning lady, Joyce, who had worked for me for years. She had a lot of health problems and was actually on welfare and Medicaid, so she wasn't supposed to be working. But she couldn't keep up with food and housing expenses. She continued with some of her favorite clients after she went on disability. I used to pay her in cash to help her avoid getting disqualified from getting welfare benefits. Remember that idiot in the last election who made tons of money putting small businesses into bankruptcy and then having the gall to refer to people accepting 'entitlements' as the 'takers'?"

"Indeed I do. It's a mystery to me how some rich people have no empathy for folks living in poverty."

"Not only do they lack empathy, they actually blame them for not working hard enough or not getting a good education. They don't seem to know that most of these folks are working two or three part time jobs so don't qualify for employer health insurance. Then they fire a bunch of their own employees and brag about how productive their remaining employees are, but don't give them a raise to reward them! Anyway, back to Joyce, who continued to work for me and a couple of other people in spite of her poor health. She was even working a second job in a diner! Slipped on some grease that had spilled on the floor, breaking a few bones in one arm and one leg. I visited her in the hospital, and she begged me to keep her job open. She fully intended to come back."

"Amazing. Did she actually come back to work?"

"Yes. I had some temporary help for a while, but it was unsatisfactory. She came back to work after about three months, but either Michael or I had to be there to tote the vacuum cleaner up and down the stairs for her. Then she ended up in the hospital again in congestive heart failure. She was discharged home, but died that same night. Her neighbor George, who was her unpaid caretaker, called me in tears, asking me to come to her funeral. He didn't want to face her siblings by himself."

"Had you met any of them before?"

"No, but Joyce used to tell me stories about family gatherings. Her sister Cassie was the alpha female of the bunch and woe be to anyone who suggested any changes to vacation plans, dinner menu or even the color of the tablecloth. Her other sister, Sue Ann, was apparently more amiable but no match for Cassie. Brother Duwayne was somewhat more tolerable, and often took Joyce on fishing expeditions, her favorite sport. He was also on disability because of a bad back. Joyce thought he was probably hooked on a combination of pain pills and alcohol. At any rate I had a heckuva time trying to find the Pine Grove cemetery, which turned out to be hidden from the surrounding cornfields by shrubs and trees. When I finally found it, the graveside ceremony was already in progress. I tried not too successfully to blend in with the dozen or so mourners. Cassie spotted me immediately as someone who was not a member of the tribe. After the ceremony, she came up and offered her hand saying, 'You must be Dr. Kepner. Joyce would be right proud to know you took time off of work to come to her funeral.'"

Kate paused. "You still awake?"

"Listening with rapt attention."

"I replied that I regretted not visiting her during her last hospitalization but she had sounded so optimistic I thought I could wait to see her after she got home. Duwayne broke in to thank me for helping fund a fishing vacation that she took with him. He also thought it was very generous of me to give her my aging Geo Prizm. I could see George lurking in the background being totally ignored by the family. He came over to greet me and then left to go home. I remembered that George had once told me he was designated to see to it she was cremated and her ashes scattered over Lake Erie, one of her favorite fishing spots."

"I can see where this is headed," laughed Anna.

"So I asked Duwayne, who must've known about her desire to join her beloved fish, why she had not been cremated. Sue Ann tried to say something but Cassie took over again. She let us know in no uncertain terms that

Joyce could not have been serious about cremation."

Kate did a credible imitation of an Appalachian accent: "It just ain't the Christian thang to do. Why, come resurrection day . . . where would she be? Oh, George tried to talk us out of a proper funeral, but he ain't family, and he wasn't to pay for it anyway. So we done the right thang."

Kate continued her narrative in a normal voice. "Sue Ann mustered enough courage to invite me to come back to Joyce's house for some refreshments. I pleaded guilty to having taken time off from work and said I needed to get back to the hospital."

"How could you resist?"

"I should have gone at least to protect George. Duwayne noticed that he had left and declared that George, who still had a key to Joyce's house, could not be trusted as he might have gone back to pilfer some of her possessions. So he generously offered to leave immediately and check out the house. My hunch is that he was hoping to get there before anyone else and see what he could make off with."

"I'll bet that put Cassie in a bind. She probably knows better than the others that Duwayne is the one to keep an eye on."

"That's her problem. But there is more! When I got home after the accident there was a message on the answering machine from a man who did not leave his name asking me to call him back about the Geo Prizm. It took me a while to figure out that someone must have been looking for the title to the car I had given Joyce, and that had to be Duwayne."

Anna yawned. "I'm glad you are driving. I'm getting highway hypnosis despite all this drama. I look for another chapter tomorrow."

"There won't be another chapter. I blocked the number so I don't expect to hear from him again. He can duke it out with George, but he will lose. I recall that when we did the title transfer, George was listed as a co-owner, so he probably already has the title and the keys to the car."

Anna laughed. "I like happy endings."

The Norovirus

The two schemers arrived in Columbus around 5 PM. After a quick meal, Kate announced that she had decided to take a few more days of vacation to visit her sister who lived in Muncie, Indiana. She hadn't seen her for a year, and with the new job looming on the horizon this was the best time for a visit.

"Is this the sister whose husband had the auto accident and became quadriplegic?" inquired Anna.

"Yes, but he died three years ago," replied Kate. "Mary finally managed to get some education, find a job and develop a social life for the first time since high school. So now she is hooked up with someone she met on line. They bought a house together and are living happily in sin. A few months ago he developed jaundice and it came to light that he was a pretty heavy drinker."

"How sad," observed Anna. "She probably never had a chance to develop any street smarts."

"What is really sad is that someone at the University Hospital decided he was a candidate for a liver transplant and now all her time is consumed with preparations for that."

"How does an alcoholic qualify for a transplant?" Anna inquired.

"He has to be off the sauce for six months and have two people confirmed and committed as caregivers. Mary has agreed to be one even though they are not married. None of his relatives are willing to commit to be back-up."

"Well, six months is not a reasonable criterion," Anna snorted. "The pattern for most alcoholics is alternating periods of sobriety and getting smashed."

"Of course. But who listens to us? At any rate, her house is a mess with all the medical appointments taking her time. I offered to come by and help her shovel out the debris."

After a quick snack, Kate sped off for Indiana while Anna sat down to get her to-do lists ready for the next day. The first hurdle was picking a date. Anna's birthdate was September 2nd, but that turned out to be too close to Labor Day which was on September 1st. She settled on the following weekend, so as not to compete with late summer vacation plans, and sent a text to Kate to see if that date was all right. Arrivals could come on Friday evening or Saturday morning. Motel reservations would be made for one evening. The treasure hunt would begin early Saturday afternoon whenever guests were all assembled. Anna estimated that the hunt would last approximately two hours, which dictated that the libations would have to be set out by 3:30 PM, and the picnic would start around 4 PM. She made a note to send an email to Michael regarding the picnic menu.

Another sensitive subject was finding out who was currently married to whom, or who was just co-habiting. Might there be some other same-sex couples that they hadn't heard about? Anna recently had an embarrassing experience while congratulating an acquaintance on his upcoming marriage to "Jody" whose daughter was to be the flower girl for the ceremony. Anna had inquired if they looked forward to adding to the family, only to learn the Jody was a man. A list of names from the Medical School could not reliably define the relationship or gender. Life was getting complicated, especially now that the medical community seemed to agree that there is a biological basis for transgender diagnosis and treatment. She would make discreet inquiries to mutual friends to clarify such matters.

The next day she had information from the alumni and development offices, which had generated a list of 24 addresses and emails accounting for 35 individuals. "I'd better run those names by Kate one more time,'" she muttered to herself. After checking several motels in the area, she decided to use the Leisure Time Inn which was about $100/night. Rooms could be reserved at the airport facility for those who flew in, and there was another one at an exit from I-71 for those who drove. Later she drove around the neighborhood looking for clever places for the treasure hunt, and made more notes on creative clues that could be used to guide and confound the participants. The next day, she set to work creating a draft of the invitations on her computer.

The following day when she was ready to call Kate with an update, the phone rang. It was Kate. "Hey there. Are you finished cleaning the Augean stables? Could you come back via Columbus?" asked Anna.

Kate's voice was an octave lower than her normal soprano. "I'm in the hospital." A long silence, then, "I was staying in a hotel since there was no room at Mary's even after we got rid of five trash bags of junk. The woman had 400 pairs of shoes, for God's sake!"

"Huh." Anna heard that as Kate's customary hyperbole.

"No, seriously. We got it down to 100 pairs. Don't even ask about the other junk. If she can't find something, she just buys another whatever. Who needs three rolling pins? I use a wine bottle. She bought one of those TV-advertised exercise machines which she can't use because she has asthma and arthritis. Never bought a vacuum cleaner though. Give a girl raised in poverty a job and a credit card and this is what you get. We finally cleared a space to set up a bed for her. Bob decided he liked it better than his hospital bed. I almost assassinated him. He can't even take an extra step to throw a jar into the recycle bin. Says he'll do it later. Puts it on the counter. 'Later' is a house full of shit that could win a prize on the Hoarders TV show . . .and a depressed caregiver. I found a used vacuum cleaner for $46 and bought it for her now that there is room to use it."

"The hospital?" Anna prompted.

"I felt sick yesterday, but made it to the hotel after leaving Mary's house. Then I started vomiting before I even got out of the car. It became projectile. So I spent the night sitting on the toilet while heaving into the waste basket. When I got up to get into bed, I was so weak I fell down. I crawled to the phone and called Mary. She came to the hotel and called the squad. Turns out I was not only dehydrated, but the electrolytes were all screwed up and my heart had gone into atrial fibrillation."

"Good grief." Anna exclaimed while thinking, 'Why am I not surprised?' Kate was a survivor of Guillain-Barré syndrome, a mysterious autoimmune disorder of the central nervous system that caused temporary paralysis. After that she underwent surgery and chemotherapy for breast cancer. Kate no longer took medications for these conditions, but had a nightly ritual involving eye drops for glaucoma and setting up her CPAP machine for sleep apnea.

"The emergency hospital got me started on rehydration and gave me an injection which converted the atrial fibrillation back to normal sinus rhythm. Then they had to transfer me to a full service hospital for a cardiology consultation. The cardiologist came in this morning accompanied by a flock of doclings in training, poring over my cardiac tests. They discussed whether or not I should start taking Coumadin just in case the atrial fibrillation should return."

Anna hazarded an opinion. "I hope you said no."

"Of course I refused. With my luck I would trip over the cord to the CPAP machine, hit my head on the dresser and die of a cerebral bleed. Or worse, survive with permanent brain damage. Well anyway, I am not coming back via Columbus. Michael is flying out to help me drive home. By the time he gets here I should be down to only one BM per hour. I hope they let me take something other than ice water this morning."

"That sounds like a good plan. You should not drive by yourself. Give me a call when you get home and recover. I will send you the information on possible invitees by email and we can flesh out the plans later. I should be able to get the invitations out by the middle of June."

"OK. Talk to you later. I see the vampires are on their way to check my electrolytes again."

Anna hung up the phone and sighed. "That woman must have nineteen lives," she thought.

Constructing Clues

After confirming that both Kate and Michael could come the second week of September, the invitations were sent out with back up emails. Kate's new job would not start until the following week, and Michael had switched to substitute teaching so he could devote more time to a variety of liberal causes such as Occupy Wall Street and Peace in the Mideast. A week after the invitations were mailed, an ecstatic Anna called Kate.

"We have liftoff!" she shouted. "Seven yes's and only two regrets so far."

"Which ones are coming?"

"Dave Brunk is coming alone. I think he is between wives. Pat Soffit is coming with husband Ted Haney. Also Chuck Novak and Jules and Sarah Filstein. Carlos Castillo and wife are maybes. Harvey Schulman emailed profound regrets. He and his wife will be in Spain and will not return until the 15th of September. He really would like to see the gang again and is even considering an early return if it won't cost too much to make a change. Dominic is in hospice and his wife thought travel would not be wise. Chuck Novak's wife has Alzheimer's, but he may have found a caregiver to stay with her."

"I'm glad Jules can make it." said Kate. "He was the best one in the Infectious Diseases Division. I would often get depressed doing resurrection consultations on people with terminal cancer and unexplained fever. Usually, the infection was some bizarre organism resistant to everything in the book, and even if we could find something that might work, they weren't going to survive more than a few more days anyway. Jules had a way of making me feel I had something to offer even if it was not a cure."

"Yes, he is a gentleman in the classic sense of the word. He could disagree without being disagreeable. Pat had an interesting request."

"Pat is the one with the house-husband, right?"

"Yes. She and Ted are coming, but Ted wants to bring a guest along to the party. She said to forget about reserving a room. They will get a two-bedroom suite at the Marriott. It's not clear if the guest is an intimate partner or just one of his many friends in the artist community he enjoys."

At this point Michael could be heard shouting something in the background. Anna could identify only some obscenities.

"Michael doesn't want any gays at the party?" she asked.

"Relax, Anna. He is fine with gays, but he can't tolerate another man in the house who can cook. He just said if anyone tries to invade the kitchen and interfere with his custom designed menu, he will cut their fucking hands off with the cleaver ordinarily reserved for dismembering poultry. By the way, I should warn you that one of our three suitcases will be full of his special utensils and pots plus spices you have never heard of."

"That reminds me. Can he do kosher dishes? Jule's wife is strictly observant, although he is flexible when she is not around. I remember one time I invited them to a dinner party and she kept calling me to ask what was being prepared and how. As it turned out, my amateur chef did know how to prepare kosher food, but she didn't trust him.

I finally told her to come to enjoy the fellowship and I would have plenty of fresh fruits and vegetables on new plastic plates just for her."

"Yes, Michael is used to preparing kosher for our friends here in Knoxville. What else do we have to plan?"

"We need to work on the clues. I found a good way to design a treasure hunt that seems pretty popular. You hide some wooden letterboxes in various places and give the contestants a list of clues. The letterboxes have a stamp inside which they will use to verify their list of clues."

The two conspirators spent an hour on the phone constructing the wording of the clues . . . not so simple that everyone could guess immediately, yet not as obtuse as a Delphic oracle. A map would be created with clearly identified landmarks (banks, churches, restaurants, grocery stores, parks and municipal buildings.) No boxes would be hidden inside any high traffic buildings, nor near any merchandise for sale. Private residences would be off limits of course. The last clue should be somewhere near Anna's home so that the guests would eventually converge to participate in the celebratory picnic.

Kate regretted that there was no nearby cemetery, having already constructed a clue that read, *Abandon all hope all ye who enter!* Anna thought that was a perfect clue for a local hospital, but none of them had free parking so those choices were crossed off the list. Strip malls would be better since there were always parking spaces available. She was enthusiastic about a small kid's park near the fire station on Reed Road. A clue directing contestants to the park was taken from Stevenson's poem about swinging: *Oh I do think it's the loveliest thing, ever a child can do.*

The entrance to her home in Concord Village usually had very little traffic so it would be possible to use the welcome sign as a clue directing the lucky detectives to the last letterbox without creating a traffic snarl. The clue would be a variation of the famous line from the poem about Paul's ride to Concord Massachusetts: *One if by land and two if by sea, and I on the opposite curb will be.*

A tentative route was drafted, using public places or vendors where Anna had contacts with employees willing to cooperate.

Station 1: The AT&T store on Reed and Henderson.
Station 2: The newspaper vending machine in front of the branch post office
Station 3: The Animal Clinic on Dierker Rd.
Station 4: The Ali Baba restaurant
Station 5: The kiddie park by the Fire Station
Station 6: The Concord Village sign
Station 7: The Fifth Third Bank on Dierker Rd.

"I'll keep working on other places we can use and let you know what works out. If you think of a clever clue, let me know and I will try to find the appropriate place," said Anna.

"OK. Keep me posted on the replies."

Anna was now thoroughly engaged in the project. Somewhat adept with graphic software, she spent more time than she could really spare designing the clues using elaborate images reminiscent of the Lord of the Rings and Harry Potter. "Damn, this is really fun," she thought. "Wish I could invite fifty people."

By the middle of August Anna found that her 50% rule was way off. Of the twenty nine potential guests twelve had already accepted, and if Harvey decided to return early from Spain there would be thirteen. She had yet to hear from several invitees. Four couples so far were going to drive in. It was not clear if Pat's husband and friend were going to participate in the hunt, or if they saw this as an opportunity to create their own special adventure away from censorious eyes. She was also having a problem thinking of appropriate prizes for the winner. Anna's tendency to obsess over details was derided by Kate during one of their many telephone marathons.

"Chill out. You don't have to worry about the picnic. Michael always cooks twice as much as is needed anyway. He will do the grocery shopping. I will be your go-fer person. If you really have to freak out about something, reserve some parking spots near your house from the neighbors. Here are my ideas on prizes. Since all of us already have too many "things", maybe a book or video on how to get rid of stuff. I think George Carlin did a show on that a few years back."

Anna said, "I saw that Carlin video a few years ago. It was pretty good. Or how about a free consultation? It's a well-known fact that physicians rarely follow their own advice, especially when it comes to mental health. How about asking someone in the psych department to give a free counseling session via Skype on the personal conflict of their choice?"

"Nix on the counseling idea. The winner probably wouldn't use it, even if they needed it. I predict Dave will be the winner. He has always been very competitive, and not one to think he needs any help with personal problems.

I have always wondered if he had marital counseling before his 3rd divorce. Maybe we should just keep it simple and give a month's supply of Cialis or a box of panty liners to the winner."

There was a pause during which both friends simultaneously realized a slight flaw in their plans. The prize could not be gender specific. Kate brought up another issue.

"You know, it may not be a good idea to have ten or more cars driven by people who may have cataracts or macular degeneration hurtling through unfamiliar streets while trying to beat the clock. Why don't we create teams of three or four so they can collaborate on interpreting the clues and reading the road map, leaving the driver to just concentrate on not mowing down one of the locals?"

"Great idea, Kate. Should we create the teams or have them draw straws?"

"Well either way there is going to be an argument about which car to use and who will do the driving. I'm pretty sure Dave will be driving something small and exotic. And don't forget that one person in each car will have to be the designated GPS monitor. But to keep arguments to a minimum, have them draw numbered slips of paper. All the "ones" are a team, and so on until you have everyone accounted for. You might even find some teams are all one gender."

"What a thought. Can you imagine four men in one car agreeing on how to get to a particular destination? I have a vision of three cell phones used to find driving directions which are all different."

"So we just award a prize to the winning team. How about a donation of $100 to their chosen charity? Or political candidate? Or voucher to pay for any speeding tickets?

Anna chuckled. "Oh I can just see the eruption in your household when Michael finds out you have made a donation supporting someone's Republican Senator."

"Not to worry. We can't participate in the hunt. Anyway, we have one joint account for household expenses and taxes in addition to separate personal accounts to use as we wish. Hardly a week goes by without Michael threatening to chain himself to the White House fence over something Obama has failed to do. Right now he is angry that the Democratic candidates do not want Obama around on the campaign trail because he is so unpopular. Michael thinks he should do some fireside chats like FDR used to do to remind people of all the things government has done for the 47%. I told him that fence chaining is so old school. He should just jump the fence. The way things are going with the Secret Service he could probably make it all the way into the Oval Office and give Obama his advice personally."

"I like the idea of a simple cash prize if they could agree on a charity. Maybe a bottle of champagne for each contestant? No teetotalers in this bunch. How about a booby prize for the last car in? Which reminds me, what is the criterion for winning? Fastest time to locate all letterboxes? Fewest false stops?"

"Well we don't want people crashing into each other when trying to park near your house and get in the door. Probably should have them record start time and time of finding the last letterbox on their clue lists," replied Kate. "And I am tempted to offer a penalty ticket to the losing team assigning them to cleanup duty."

Anna laughed. "Let's put this on hold for a while. Maybe the creative juices will start flowing again tomorrow."

Kate said, "Speaking of creative juices . . . I'm going to fix myself a Bloody Mary!"

"That's the best idea I've heard today!"

Fourteen and Counting

Feeling somewhat anxious and in need of compassionate hand-holding, Anna called Kate to give her the latest update. "Tell Michael we have fourteen plus the three of us for a total of seventeen so far. But I am still waiting for seven or eight replies. Jean Chang asked if it would be okay to bring a guest at the last minute. I told her if she needed a date Dave was probably available. She was not amused."

Kate chuckled. "Have you forgotten the flap she and Dave had? They were both involved in taking care of a patient who developed post-operative confusion and fever. She was the primary care physician and Dave was called by the surgeon because the serum electrolytes were messed up. Since the urine output appeared to be good, Dave did not at first realize the patient was dehydrated and did not adjust the IV solutions. Jean determined that the fever was due to a lung infection and started the first round of antibiotics. She also noticed that the urine was abnormally dilute for someone who was clearly dehydrated as judged by the poor elasticity of the skin. So she called Dave and said she thought the patient had diabetes insipidus. This to a kidney specialist! Of course that was a blow to his ego. Then she drove the proverbial knife in a little deeper by saying, 'Of course you know he takes lithium so it is probably nephrogenic diabetes insipidus.'"

"Yes," Anna interjected. "It's always humiliating to hear the nursing staff telling stories about your bloopers. Do you think there could be some bad chemistry here?"

"Hey, it's up to them to decide how to handle bygones. We have all had our share of eating humble pie. I got teased mercilessly about the time a resident called me to see a patient in the emergency room. He had a penile lesion which the resident thought was primary syphilis. He was pretty excited about that diagnosis since we don't see much of that anymore."

"No kidding. That would call for a general viewing by the entire contingent of medical students assigned to the hospital!"

"Well, when I finished making rounds with the general medicine residents I was way behind on my schedule. I went roaring down to the emergency room and told the nurse that I had been asked to see a patient, giving her the name that I had scribbled down. I found an elderly man hooked up to an IV and after a few questions it was clear he was not playing with a full deck of cards. I said to myself, 'If this man has syphilis, it's likely to be tertiary not primary.'"

"You can't assume anything. I hear sexually transmitted diseases are not unusual in retirement villages."

"Point taken. But I went ahead and asked a few questions including the mandatory ones about sexual behavior. He did seem to understand those, saying, 'Honey, I wish I could say I have been playing around, but I haven't been able to get it up for 10 years.' However, he didn't seem to mind having his private parts examined. When I failed to see any skin lesions down there, I was puzzled but went back to the nurse's station to write up the consultation."

"Now there is a red alert if ever I heard one."

"Hind sight is always perfect. Halfway through the note I noticed that the name of the doctor who had called me for a consultation was not on the chart. Nor did the notes indicate that an infectious disease consultation was requested. To make a long story short, I called the resident and found out that he had called from the Good Sam hospital, not Miami Valley where I had been making rounds. What are the odds of both of the hospitals having a man with the same name in the ER at the same time! So of course I had to cram a trip to Good Sam hospital into my already messed up schedule. The story of my mistake got to the hospital before I did."

"Well, when you finally found the right patient, did he have a syphilitic lesion?"

"As a matter of fact he did. He was a young chap who had just started college and was sampling all the good campus life without the nuisance of parental oversight. I gave him a lecture about condoms. And about appropriate uses of emergency rooms."

"Getting back to the logistics of the party, I am creating a Gantt chart starting Friday evening and working back to Monday, listing what needs to be done and when. I will email it to you and Michael tonight. Let me know of anything I should get now to make things easier for all of us."

"Omigod. A Gantt chart! Only an obsessive-compulsive, anal-retentive nerd would think of applying industrial project management to a simple party. You have a pretty good idea of who is coming; you know where they are staying. Michael will buy the food. I will buy the booze. All you have to do is count how many plates, forks, glasses, and napkins you need, and make sure you have plenty of toilet paper. If you feel obliged to make it complicated, figure out how many Tums you will need to treat the inevitable heartburn . . . and where to put the bodies who are not fit to drive back to their hotels."

"Well, that could be just about everyone. Maybe I should hire some designated drivers."

"Not a bad idea," said Kate. "Why don't you hire your son? He would probably be amused to watch dignified professionals making fools of themselves. Maybe he could hook up with Jean Chang. She's not that much older than he is."

Anna hung up the phone feeling reassured. She consulted her RSVP list again. There were still some people who had not responded. Jim and Dena Atkins, both family practitioners, had been close friends when she lived in Dayton and still exchanged Christmas cards with her, so it was odd that they hadn't replied. She was not as close with the Wheelers: Rob, a specialist in infectious diseases, and his wife Joy, a specialist in physical medicine. Because they were good friends of Kate's, also an infectious diseases specialist, she had expected a prompt reply. Beth Fowler, a psychotherapist, was never very reliable about replying, so that was not unusual. Her ex-husband Roger had not replied either. He was a retired minister who later got his tickets as a counselor and had joined Beth in doing couple's therapy. She was not sure if the addresses she had been given for them were correct, but no mail had been returned. Chuck Novak, a jazz musician masquerading as a dermatologist, would be great fun if he decided to come. He was the target of constant ribbing by other faculty members who never failed to ask him how many nighttime emergencies he had attended in the past week. And he never failed to reply with a story about a fictitious patient with a terminal form of lichen planus or genital warts.

Sumei, her Burmese cat, emerged from his favorite nap site: a dark corner in the coat closet next to her small office. He could always count on a scarf or jacket slipping to the floor and offering a warm, cozy place to hibernate. After yawning and stretching, he padded after Anna who had gone out to the patio to pick some tomatoes and lettuce for lunch. Hearing his soft bass growl, she leaned over to scratch him under the chin. "Back in the house, Sumei," she ordered. "I don't want to see any more chipmunk parts brought into the living room."

The Doberman

Wednesday, September 3, 2014, dawned to find an anxious Anna emailing the latest update to Kate and Michael.

> Just got word that the Wheelers returned from Africa last month. They had volunteered with Doctors Without Borders to work in a village devastated by the Ebola epidemic. They voluntarily quarantined themselves at home for a few weeks as an extra precaution. They are good to go and will arrive Friday night from Colorado. Rob asked if they should bring some pot, since sale is not legal in Ohio. I said as long as they didn't bring Ebola they could bring anything they wanted. Jim and Dena were trying to work around a family wedding (which promises to be a debacle because one of the mothers thinks she is in charge of all arrangements) but decided they couldn't come. Chuck is coming after all and probably has his own supply of pot! I still haven't heard from Beth. I sent a last minute invitation to Fred and Sue Fisert. No reply. Chuck thinks Fred may have died recently. Carlos Castillo and his wife Peggy are coming. So the count now is eighteen plus the three of us. Woo-hoo! I trust you are coming in on Thursday the 4th, which is tomorrow??

It was time to consult the Gantt chart again, murmuring happily as she made notes. "Probably need a new tank of propane for the grill. Will need to find two extra folding tables in addition to the picnic table; fresh flowers would be nice for the inside; and I should get some yellow crime scene tape to cordon off the kitchen area from the guests." Her condo featured one great room which began at the front door and extended to the patio door. Only the bedrooms and bathrooms had interior walls and doors. The tape was more to protect the guests from Michael than vice-versa. However she didn't know where to buy it and at this point didn't have time to do any research.

As she was putting some final notes on the Gantt chart, she got a call from Karen, a friend who was supposed to conduct an orientation for their time bank. Anna was one of the founders of the local time bank, a community of people who exchange services instead of paying for them. The meeting was scheduled for 7 o'clock that evening. Would Anna take her place please, please, please? Karen had to make an emergency trip to Cleveland because her mother was in the hospital. That was the last thing Anna wanted to do two days before a big event. However she had leaned heavily on Karen to take on this responsibility, assuring her that there was plenty of back-up.

Trying to sound cheerful through grinding teeth, Anna said, "Of course I can do it tonight. You need to be in Cleveland. Go!"

Tossing aside the chart, she dug through her files in her little office, which desperately needed to be de-cluttered to make space for the party supplies. She found the orientation files, pulled out the projector and laptop, quickly checking the supplies. The power cord to the projector was missing. That meant a quick trip to Micro Center while praying that a compatible cord could be found. The crime scene tape would have to be scratched off the to-do list. The Gantt chart said she should be vacuuming the house and washing the kitchen floor at 1 PM. Instead, she was on her way to the church to make twenty copies of each of the handouts she would need that evening. Her printer had informed her that the ink cartridge was almost nil. While standing at the copier she called some of the time bank members.

"Chris, I know this is short notice but could you come over early tomorrow morning and help me clean the house? I have a big party this weekend but I have been sidetracked by having to do a time bank orientation tonight."

"Gosh, I'm sorry but I don't have a minute to spare for the next three days."

Three more calls were equally unproductive. A church member who was also a member of the time bank walked into the copy room. "Hi Anna, what's up?"

"Well hi there, Jason. I'm trying to find someone help me clean my house tomorrow so I can devote my time to setting up a party for about 22 people."

"I can do that. I'd like to add two or three hours credit to my time bank account."

"I thought you joined the time bank to get people to clean your house. Why would you clean somebody else's?"

"Because my house is a god-awful mess. Yours should be a piece of cake by comparison."

"Oh Jason, that's so good of you!" She scribbled her address onto a piece of scrap paper and handed it to him. "See you tomorrow around nine or ten?"

"Sure thing."

Picking up the stack of handouts, she returned to her car and headed for the electronics store. She had forgotten to put the projector in the car but hoped the power cord was a fairly standard piece of equipment. The clerk in the media center assured her that power cords were pretty generic. She grabbed the cord, picked up a package of copy paper, printer ink, and headed for the checkout counter.

It was 3 o'clock in the afternoon when she returned home. Indeed, the power cord did fit the projector. She started stacking her electronics and all of her supplies into the rolling cart she used for such meetings. She bent over to retrieve the file containing her script and handouts. Suddenly, she felt as if a Doberman pinscher had clamped its jaws onto the right side of her back. Gasping in pain, she knelt on the floor and very slowly lowered her head and butt to the floor, stretching her arms forward. This was the "child's pose" she used in her Pilates exercises to stretch her back. After a few minutes she hoisted her rear end into the air and walked her hands backward toward her feet. Very carefully she walked her hands up her legs until she was upright again. This was definitely not on her Gantt chart. The pain was still there, but at least she was able to move. She called another time bank member for help.

"Ruth, I have an orientation meeting tonight. I know you don't need orientation, but it's useful to have some testimonials from members. Could you come tonight? I could also use some help setting up the tables and with the sign-in sheets and the handouts. You'll get two hours credit just for attending."

"Sure. I could use the hours, plus it's nice to have a refresher course on how to use the software."

"Wonderful! It's at the Reynoldsburg library. I will be there at 6:30 to set up. See you then."

Anna finished packing the cart and rolled it to the car. Lifting the heavy cart was also not in the Gantt chart. By unpacking the cart, putting it into the trunk and dumping the contents back in, she was able to avoid another muscle spasm. Returning to the kitchen, she made a sandwich and a cup of tea, washing down four Advil tablets. Careful to avoid turning her torso, she rose from the chair, slowly walked back to the garage, and opened the car door. Turning 180 degrees to the left, she sat down, lifted her feet and slowly turned her body to face forward. *So far so good,* she thought. She made one stop to pick up a few packs of bottled water and a dozen cookies, arriving at the library a little before 6:30.

It was easier to get the cart out than it was to get it in because the car was a hatch back and she didn't have to lean over to lift the cart, but she did feel a warning twinge in the lumbar area when she set the cart on the pavement. Ruth was setting up the tables and chairs classroom style. Anna started hooking together the computer, projector and speakers. This step was always accompanied by anxiety because she was never confident that all the components would cooperate with each other.

"Hooray," she exclaimed when the computer desktop appeared on the screen. "First good thing that's happened today." She walked over to help Ruth set up the handout table.

"Why are you walking sideways?" asked Ruth.

"My back decided to give me a lot of grief today. I'm fine as long as I don't twist or bend in any direction. Can you put the cookies and water on the back table?"

"Sure. Couldn't you find someone to take over for you?"

"Actually, I am taking over for Karen who had to go to Cleveland today. There wasn't time to find a second substitute."

By 7 o'clock about ten people were seated and reading the handouts. Anna began the meeting by introducing herself and inviting the attendees to say a few words about why they had come. The orientation started with a video from the PBS website: a documentary about a time bank in Portland Maine. She then went through a PowerPoint presentation about the local time bank and then went online to demonstrate how the software worked. The rest of the meeting consisted of answering questions. By 8:15 things were winding down and the Advil was beginning to wear off. She and Ruth packed up all of the supplies. Another longtime member who had attended the meeting to get more credits, helped put everything into the car for her.

"Why are you walking sideways?" he asked.

"It's a long story," she said. "Let's just say that my back has outlived its usefulness."

"I know all about that," he replied. "Maybe you could get a massage from one of the time bank members."

"Actually, I plan to call my favorite Chinese masseuse tomorrow morning."

By the time Anna returned home the Doberman was gnawing on her back mercilessly. Poking through the medicine cabinet, she found a small vial of codeine tablets that had been prescribed two years earlier after a root canal. She had only taken one or two of the tablets at that time. Hoping that the chemicals had not deteriorated into something lethal, she washed down two tablets. A half hour later she decided they had lost a lot of potency and took two more. By 10 o'clock she had fallen into a troubled sleep. At 11 o'clock the phone rang.

"Whoozz zis?" She managed to get out through lips that refused to move.

"Anna? Is that you? This is Kate."

"Yesh shmee," she managed to get out.

"What's wrong? Have you been drinking?"

By this time Anna was awake but her tongue was still not moving properly. She tried to explain without much success.

"You've been attacked by a Doberman?" asked an astounded Kate.

For a while, no useful information was exchanged. Then Kate extracted a few coherent facts from Anna's garbled speech. Most important was that Anna was in no condition to plan anything much less a party for 20+ people. Kate had called to say that she and Michael expected to arrive the following day late at night instead of the afternoon as originally planned. She decided not to alarm Anna, telling her to go back to sleep and she would call again in the morning.

Kate ended the call and headed for Michael's study, expecting to find him posting more insulting anti-Republican cartoons on his Facebook page. Instead she found him poring over cookbooks and scribbling notes. Peering over his shoulder, she saw items like crostini with chopped chicken liver, eggplant with anchovy paste, lobster ravioli, Neapolitan tart, orzo with grilled shrimp, summer vegetables, pesto vinaigrette, amaretto biscotti.

"Whatever are you doing at this hour?" She asked.

"I'm preparing a grocery list for Anna's party."

"Looks like an Italian wedding banquet. What's wrong with a standard American picnic menu?"

"Hey, I'm Italian. This is a special birthday party for your best friend. I'm not going to make boring American food."

"Well my best friend happens to be Polish. I have her recipe for nalesniki. Want to try that?"

"Those are crêpes aren't they? I'll do that for breakfast."

Kate took a deep breath. This was going to be a difficult negotiation. "We may have to change our plans tomorrow. Anna sprained something in her back today and she is currently laid up in bed stoned on codeine. If we arrive late tomorrow night, there may not be time to get everything ready by Friday evening when the first guests arrive."

Michael looked up, frowning. "You want us to leave before the fundraiser? You know I organized it for the initiative to get that idiot off the school board. I have to be there."

"I want to get there in time to see if she needs medical attention and make sure the party isn't a disaster."

"These medical adventures are supposed to happen to you, not Anna." He was clearly avoiding a decision that would make one of them very unhappy.

"I know that you are upset about the latest school board election."

"You better believe it. There are too many creationists on it. Since that witch Brody was elected, there is a threat that the science textbooks are going to be replaced with garbage. They might even bring in that screwball from Colorado who does exorcisms on TV."

"How would you feel if I drove out in the morning by myself to do damage control, and you drove up later in your car? You could give me your grocery list so I could get the major supplies while I am buying the beverages?"

Michael looked greatly relieved. "Sure you don't mind driving alone?"

"I drove up alone a couple of months ago."

"You also ended up in the hospital and I had to fly up to drive you back home."

"Well clearly the curse has been passed onto Anna so I'm not going to get sick this time."

Michael chuckled. "Promise?"

A relieved Kate hugged Michael and left to start packing. She pulled her favorite jeans out of the drawer and put them on to make sure they still fit. She had lost quite a bit of weight during her bout with the Norovirus, but that had been mostly fluid loss and she was afraid she was back to normal plus a few pounds. Supersized from childhood, she led a life marked by periodic torture with the diet du jour followed by regaining the pounds she had so painfully shed. Happily, the jeans were a comfortable fit. She debated about packing a dress. After all, this was a reunion of friends, many of whom she had not seen for over 10 years. It called for a special celebration. Finally she decided against it. She certainly wasn't going to wear it to the picnic, and it was unlikely that many would stay for another day and night. Instead she would pair the jeans with a designer blouse and some expensive jewelry. There was a box of photograph albums on the closet floor. To her delight, she found one labeled WSU, 1998–2004. She selected one album to stuff into her suitcase and fell into bed feeling more optimistic about the party.

Walking Sideways

Anna woke up a little before 7 AM on Thursday to hear the announcer from WOSU FM tell his audience that the temperature was a balmy 76° with sunshine, but to expect light showers in the afternoon. She had the sense that today was an important day but couldn't quite figure out why. Turning to her left side, she felt a sharp pain travel down her right thigh. Then the events of the previous day began to tumble into her consciousness. She wondered if she dared get out of bed. At least the Doberman was not chewing on her back anymore. She maneuvered her knees to the edge of the mattress and slowly pushed herself into a sitting position.

"So far, so good," she muttered.

She put her feet on the floor, stood up and walked slowly into the bathroom, wincing every time she put weight on her right leg. There was diffuse soreness from the bottom of the right rib cage, down to the right buttock and the outside of her right thigh. Sitting on the toilet made this worse, but overall the pain was tolerable. She limped into the kitchen and put an extra measure of coffee into the one-cup brewer. While it was burbling away she fixed her usual bowl of Cheerios, fruit and milk, and downed a glass of orange juice along with four Advil tablets. Sumei appeared from his hideout in the office closet and growled a greeting. She cautiously took a cup of coffee to the recliner facing the TV set.

Now for some laughter therapy, she thought while switching on the TV and looking for the latest episode of the Daily Show with Jon Stewart on the DVR. Halfway through the episode she got a call from Kate.

"Well hello there," she said. "I was just going to call you. You won't believe what happened yesterday."

"You told me all about it last night." said Kate.

"What do you mean? I didn't talk to you last night."

"Well in some sense you didn't. Mainly you babbled incoherently. What I got out of the non-conversation was that you have either slipped a disk in your lumbar spine or have an industrial sized sprain of the paraspinal muscles. Or had an orgy with a Doberman."

"I told you that last night?" said an incredulous Anna. "I don't remember talking to you. Anyway, I think it's just a sprain, not a slipped disc. I don't have any numbness in my leg."

"That's a relief. Michael and I have changed our plans slightly. I am leaving in about an hour to drive myself to your house to make sure you don't end up in the hospital trying to do things you shouldn't. Michael will go to his rally in the afternoon and join us sometime before midnight."

Anna was almost speechless with relief. There was a quaver in her voice when she replied, "That is such good news. Thank you."

"Hey, that's what friends are for. Now don't do something stupid in the next few hours."

"I managed to find someone to come over this morning to clean the house. Then I'm going to see if my masseuse has an opening this morning to work the kinks out of my back."

"Now you're starting to make sense. Take care and I'll see you this afternoon."

Jason arrived a little after 9 o'clock. He surveyed the condo with a critical eye. "Well I see the breakfast dishes need doing, but the rest of the place doesn't look like it needs any real work. I should be done in an hour."

"There is more than meets the eye," said Anna while she walked him around the condo. "All these rooms need to be vacuumed, the kitchen floor needs washing, and the glass table tops need to be cleaned, plus of course dusting the furniture."

"Okay, two hours max. Why are you walking sideways?"

By this time Anna was beginning to see the humor in the whole situation. She described what happened after she left him in the copy room of the church. "So now I am off to see my Chinese masseuse whose employees have magical hands."

"Do they do acupuncture too? Maybe you should try that."

"Yes they offer all kinds of therapy. It's an interesting place. The proprietor speaks English pretty well, but there are different employees there every time I go. I have a hunch they just got off the boat. They may not be properly credentialed. Most of them have a very limited English vocabulary. I personally have no use for some of these new therapies like putting one hand on your skull and the other on your butt while telling you that their energy is flowing into your body. I prefer a heavy hand that pummels muscles into submission. That's what these guys do. A little ouchy at times, but at the end they prepare a bed of hot rocks for me to lie on, pile some more on my abdomen and chest and leave it to me how long I want to stay there. I actually feel taller when I leave."

"Sounds like there may be some illegal stuff going on there. Have they ever offered you any opium?"

"Not so far, but I would have taken it last night, given the opportunity. If you get hungry or thirsty feel free to take anything in the fridge." Anna shuffled out to the car humming the tune "It's a Wonderful Day in the Neighborhood."

A few hours later, Anna left the massage parlor feeling lighter and no longer walking like a crab. She was able to turn and twist freely with only minor twinges in her back. Pulling the cell phone out of her purse, she unmuted it and saw that there were several voice mails waiting for her noting arrival information. Some would arrive Saturday, mainly those driving in from nearby cities like Dayton (Chuck Novak, Dave Brunk, and the Magees) and Cincinnati (Vivian Rogers). Jean Chang, who now lived in Arizona, wanted to come on Friday evening and asked for two night's accommodation at the motel. Pat Soffit and her entourage also planned to arrive Friday so they could attend a performance at the Ohio Theatre that evening. They offered to come early on Saturday and help set things up. Harvey Schulman planned to fly in to Cincinnati on Friday and drive in with Vivian the next day. Anna made a mental note to jot this information into her Gantt chart when she got home. First she had to stop at a Dollar General store to purchase a couple of boxes of individual paper towels to place in the bathrooms. Nobody wants to re-use cloth hand towels these days, especially physicians.

When she returned home, she found that Jason had indeed done a good job of cleaning up the house. He was seated in her favorite recliner chair watching TV and drinking a beer.

"I decided to take you up on the offer to raid the refrigerator. The lasagna was great."

"Well," replied Anna, "you have certainly earned it. Did anyone call on the landline?"

"There were a few calls but only one left a message. Sounded like a debt collector. And all this time I thought you were an upstanding responsible citizen."

"When I moved here two years ago, I was given a new phone number. Clearly the person who had it before was a deadbeat. How many hours shall I credit you for cleaning up the house?"

"Two would be fine. You have a leaky faucet in the master bathroom. I tried to fix it with a new washer but it looks like you're going to have to get a new faucet. If you decide to buy a new one let me know and I will install it for you."

"After this party is over, I may have a whole bunch of repairs for you to work on!"

Jason pitched the empty beer bottle into the recycle bin and chuckled. "Did you tell me that a dozen or more of your guests are physicians? That's a lot of big egos to put into one small condo."

"Indeed. On top of that I'm going to send them on a treasure hunt around the neighborhood. Doctors love detective stories, and you know, the work of doctoring is very similar to that of a police detective. You start out with a few clues, like symptoms and physical findings, and then, looking for the most probable diagnosis, order laboratory tests, imaging studies etc. If you are lucky, you get the right diagnosis. If not, you start digging for more clues and more ways to investigate them. Some of what you find leads you down a blind alley. Sometimes you think you have made the right diagnosis, only to find a year or two later you were wrong."

"Then you get sued, right?"

"Actually, not as often as you might think. If you communicate well with the patient, and are honest about what you know and don't know, most are pretty forgiving. Now if you do something really stupid that is preventable, like amputating the wrong leg, that's clearly grounds for a lawsuit. Other reasons are a lot murkier. Now that genetic testing is available, some couples, especially those who have genetic defects in their family tree, ask for amniotic fluid testing for genetic defects. There are a couple high profile cases of "wrongful birth" resulting in multi-million-dollar settlements. Apparently the genetic defect was missed by the laboratory and the children who were born developed full blown disabling neurologic conditions. The success of the lawsuits rested on the parents' testimony that had they been given accurate information they would have sought an abortion."

"Wow. That would make one think twice about going to medical school these days."

"I think this type of lawsuit would be less frequent if we had a rational health care system. What drove these parents to seek damages was the knowledge that they would be facing exorbitant medical expenses. Insurance companies go to great lengths to avoid offering coverage for these families. The current law, derisively referred to as Obamacare, has eliminated a lot of these insurance abuses. But the opposition party is determined to either repeal it or defund it. It's a mystery to me why they think taking health insurance away from people with low to mid-level incomes is a defensible policy."

"So, are you still working with that 'Medicare For All' outfit?"

"Yes I am. It's going to be a long haul. The politicians in Ohio's governor's office and general assembly are mostly hostile to any policy they consider socialist. The same has been true at the national level, and it is probably going to be even worse after this midterm election. Our only hope is that if Vermont manages to implement such a policy at the state level, the other states will follow. We are optimistic that can happen."

"Well, good luck. I'd better get back home."

While Anna was jotting the latest updates into her Gantt chart, she received a text from Kate stating that she had just crossed the Ohio River and should be in Columbus in a couple of hours. Then she checked the emails that had accumulated over the past two days. One was a message from Beth Fowler that didn't make any sense.

> Was thrilled to get your invitation. It would be great to see old friends again. Have moved around a bit since Roger and I broke up. Currently living in North Carolina. Am vacationing in Bermuda. We will return home tomorrow.

Now isn't that enlightening, Anna thought. *Nice to know that she will be back in North Carolina, but is she actually coming? When? And who is "we"?* She decided to not make any reservations just yet, and sent a reply:

> Good to hear from you. Need to know when you are arriving so I can make a reservation. Also need a headcount. My phone number, is 614 267 3910.

She did a quick check of the guest bedroom, clearing some books off the bedside stand so that Michael would have a place for his laptop. She glanced at her watch. Kate should arrive any minute.

Game Plans

As promised by WOSU FM, a light rain was falling as Kate pulled into the driveway about 3:30 PM. She wheeled her suitcase to the front door, which opened before she could even ring the doorbell.

"Oh it is so good to see you," said Anna. "Let me help you bring things in."

Kate gave her a gentle hug. "Don't you dare lift a thing. I don't want to find myself running this whole show while you are in the hospital in traction. Is it supposed to rain all weekend?"

"No. It's supposed to clear up before noon tomorrow. We should be able to start planting some of the clues later this afternoon. Of course we'll have to check again on Saturday to make sure they are still there. I have extra boxes and stamps just in case."

"Have you planned any get together with the ones who are coming in on Friday?"

"Nothing formal. Arrival times are all over the map. Some won't even get in till midnight. I sent them an email saying anyone who gets in by 6 PM should call me and tell me what kind of pizza they would like. We can make a salad to go with it. Should be able to eat out on the patio."

"Sounds like a plan. What should we do today?"

"Bring the rest of your stuff in and park it in the guest room. Then we can sit down and finalize the hunt. We might even drive around to see if we need to make any changes on the sites I have tentatively chosen."

While Kate was getting her supplies settled in the guest room, Anna laid out her plans for the treasure hunt on the coffee table in the living room.

"Here's what I think will work best," she told Kate as they hunched over the coffee table. "There are many different kinds of treasure hunts. I like the letterbox idea best. I bought these small wooden boxes and stamps in a hobby store. Instead of planting a clue in each box that leads them to the next box and clue, we will give each team a list of all the clues and instructions to look for the letterbox. I have put a picture of the letterbox on the first page. They can look for the boxes in any order they wish. When they find one, they will stamp a page on their list. Each stamp is different so we know who found what."

"Might be a good idea to have each team sign the notepad in the letterbox."

"Good thought. Murphy's law says that if anything can go wrong, it will."

"I like the variant that says, "If there are two or more ways to do something, and one of those ways can result in a catastrophe or pregnancy, then someone will do it."

Anna laughed. "Well at least this crowd doesn't have to worry about pregnancy!"

"So the trick is to find a place to hide the letterbox and hope somebody else doesn't remove it before the hunt begins, right?"

"Yes there is that risk, so I guess the winner is the one who finds the most letterboxes."

They spent the next hour driving around the route that Anna had designed, looking for places where the letterboxes could be hidden and thinking of the most appropriate clues for each place. On the way home they stopped for lunch at Anna's favorite Mideast restaurant, site of one of the clues. While at the Ali Baba, she talked to the proprietor about where to put the letterbox. He suggested that since placing the letterbox on top of the dessert display case could interfere with customer traffic, he would alert the manager, Samira, about the game and they would put a little sign on the dessert case that said *See manager for letters*. That sounded like a great idea."

"How's this for a clue?" said Kate.

> *Open Sesame won't unlock this door*
> *Where 40 thieves have been before*
> *When paying for your baklava*
> *Request your mail from Samira.*

"Perfect. Now let's go to the small animal clinic. That is where I take Sumei for his shots. Dr. Kline said they would be happy to help."

Upon arrival at the clinic, devoted exclusively to feline care and appropriately named "Just Cats," the receptionist said she would place the letterbox on the floor under her desk. Dr. Kline even suggested a clue: *I offer cat scans*.

The two conspirators left for the wireless phone store, happy that at least two boxes were in a secure place for the night. It took a little persuading at the ATT phone store to get cooperation. The manager agreed to accept the letterbox but did not think it would be possible to leave it inside the store. However she promised to keep it inside overnight and place it in the shrubbery by the front door in the morning. The clue would show an image of Don Adams, the actor who played Maxwell Smart, hiding in a bush and holding his shoe to his ear. The caption would read: *Get Smart . . . use the Cingularly best network*. Anna was amused to hear a sweet young thing at the store ask,

"Who is Maxwell Smart?" That should not be a problem with the generation she was hosting.

The playground near the fire station proved problematic. There were dozens of kids running around there during the week, and there would be more on Saturday, making the playground equipment unsuitable as a hiding place.

"We need to come up with a better plan," said Anna, "but I do regret not being able to use the poem about swings as a clue."

Kate looked at the adjacent fire station. "Do you think that could be a place? It would be easy to come up with a clue for that."

Entering the firehouse, they found two men concentrating on a game of checkers and another much younger one reading *Sports Illustrated*. He looked up and inquired, "What can we do for you ladies?"

Anna replied, "Hi, I'm Anna Zendzian and I live nearby in Concord Village. My friend and I are planning sort of a class reunion on Saturday and are organizing a treasure hunt. We wonder if you would allow us to place the box for clues in or near the firehouse."

He looked amused. "I thought that was for kids, and if I may say so, it looks like you two graduated quite a while ago."

Kate laughed. "Maybe before you were born. Actually, these hunts appeal to all ages and some have become quite complicated and very competitive. But our guests are not a rowdy bunch; mostly physicians and nurses."

"What's involved?"

After explaining the scenario to him, Anna said, "What we need is a place to put this box, where it won't be discovered by a local resident and carried off before we are through. The hunt will start before 2 PM and should be over by 4:00."

"Well, ma'am, I will have to run this by the chief, but I have to warn you. When an emergency call comes in this place will have more commotion than a hockey game. And there won't be anyone free to help your folks for quite a while. Those fellas over there may look like they need resuscitation, but believe me, they will be in their suits and on that truck before you can finish a call to 911."

"We certainly understand that the job comes first," said Kate. "Do you get many calls in this part of town?"

"We get one or two calls for paramedics on a daily basis, but that is a smaller team. Actual fires take more manpower and are less frequent here, but if there is a big one someplace, we may get called to help other units. Let me show you around the station." He then obligingly gave them a tour of the station inside and out, pointing out places that might be used for the letterbox.

"Thanks, Doug, said Anna, "Here is my phone number. Let me know what the chief decides."

"Will do."

Returning to Anna's house they discussed possible clues, some having to do with Dalmatians, the traditional mascot of firefighters before the combustion engine replaced horses. Anna made tea, then pulled out the Gantt chart to see what remained to be done. She showed Kate the email from Beth, saying, "Who do you suppose 'we' is? Want to place any bets on whether or not she is actually coming?"

"It's hard to imagine how such a poor communicator can actually give advice to troubled people," said Kate.

"Therapists are not supposed to give advice; they are supposed to listen, and reflect back what they hear until the unsuspecting client figures out who is at fault. As Pogo once said, 'We have met the enemy and he is us.'"

"Well, not entirely. A lot of folks have toxic families. I certainly did and I needed therapy to get past those old wounds. Just look at what has happened to my sister Mary, who can't afford therapy. But I see your point. You can't recover and establish a life of your own until you are willing to break away from people who are bent on destroying you. Where next?"

Anna reviewed her list. "We have four places done now. I decided to scratch the bank idea. Lots of people raid the ATM machines on Saturday, and the branch on Henderson road didn't have good hiding places anyway. I have a good clue for a post office and we can use the branch on Henderson, which is near the ATT wireless store. We can't use the inside of the post office, but there is a newspaper vending machine outside. If the letterbox is put behind it, you can't see it, but I am planning on placing it tomorrow with a chain and padlock securing it to one of the legs of the rack. We should also delay putting out the box near the Concord Village sign until tomorrow morning."

"So that takes care of six of the boxes and clues, right?"

"Yes, but we need one more. I am working on one involving a flower shop and we should go over there now to deliver the box. I also need help with the clue for the flower shop. Then we can work on the grocery list tonight."

"I promised Michael I would get the booze today."

"Let's go to Trader Joe's. They have a great selection of wines and their prices are good."

"I agree. And while I am there I will get their lobster ravioli. That will give Michael one less thing to obsess over."

"Good idea. And let's pick out something for supper tonight."

Anna and Kate returned to the condo around 9 PM. They unloaded the car and proceeded to fix supper. Anna had chosen Scalloped Potatoes with Quattro Fromaggio, while Kate went for Chicken Sausage with corn bread. Dessert would be pecan pie with ice cream after Michael arrived. They spent the next two hours refining the clues for the treasure hunt and reminiscing about their time at WSU, while Sumei prowled around the table hoping to find stray sausage fragments. Finding none there, he followed the scent upward, leaping onto Kate's lap to explore further. He was summarily dumped back onto the floor as Kate said, "That reminds me. I need to take some Claritin right now."

Shortly before midnight, they heard a car pull into the driveway. "That must be Michael," said Kate, heading out the front door. "I'll help him bring in his stuff. Clear off the kitchen counters . . . and the floor!"

Kate returned dragging two suitcases, followed by Michael, who wore a T shirt with the logo *Make Love not War*. This slogan seemed at odds with one of the two rolling carts he pulled, filled with pots, pans and a variety of lethal looking knives.

Michael put his laptop case on a chair and gave Anna a warm hug. "Dare I ask which birthday this is?"

"You can ask, but I won't tell. Let's just say I have had a Medicare card for a few years."

"Well, I am looking forward to getting mine someday. Wish Kate had one. You wouldn't believe what that brief stay in Muncie cost! An ambulance, an emergency hospital with transfer to a full-service hospital, and a bunch of consultants. And of course the insurance company is challenging some of the services."

"Which is why we should have Medicare for everyone like Canada does. How was your fund raiser?"

"Fantastic. We had a very good turn out and got a lot of commitments from people to attend school board meetings and circulate petitions. Some board members are determined to replace textbooks that don't have reflect what we know about evolution, and we intend to challenge this at every board meeting."

"Are you hungry?" asked Kate.

"No, I had something to eat when I stopped for gas a couple of hours ago."

"Well do you have room for pecan pie with ice cream?"

"Absolutely. Do you have a Wi-Fi network, Anna? I will need to check my email."

"Of course. The network name is Dancing Queen and the password is Luv2Rhumba."

"Sounds like you are still into ballroom dancing."

"Sadly, no. I had a great partner years ago. He could have done competition, but never tried it. I suspect he could not tolerate the possibility that he would not always get first place. Then he moved to Florida. I found someone in a singles group here who could dance basic stuff, and was willing to take lessons with me."

"Was that the fellow who came with you the last time you stayed with us?"

"Yes. He was great fun. But he died of a stroke two years ago. I tried going to the local dance places alone, but the good dancers have their own partners, and the few unattached males there were terrible dancers. I'm convinced that some folks don't have the DNA to hear a rhythmic beat. Check your email later. It's dessert time."

Kate ladled out generous portions of the ice cream onto slices of pecan pie. "I guess it's time for you to start turning rocks over again, Anna. Want any chocolate syrup on top of this ice cream?"

Anna threw up her hands in mock despair. "I have decided to replace men with hobbies that don't require a partner. Like scuba diving. And yes to the chocolate syrup."

As Michael dove into the dessert, he shared his final picnic menu. In addition to an assortment of Italian starters (cheeses, crostini, and an antipasto platter), he planned to grill chicken breasts, hot dogs, hamburgers and salmon burgers. For dessert, he had already made the almond biscotti and the Génoise cake. The cake would be soaked in triple sec this evening. Italian ices would also be available.

"What, no Tiramisu?" asked Anna.

"Oh everyone expects that and it is getting too plebian for my taste."

"No salad?" asked Kate.

"Tossed salads are too messy. I will just have a platter of sliced tomatoes and cucumbers with a light vinegar and oil coating. That is really a more authentic Italian item."

"I know it's not Italian, but local corn is delicious right now. It would go well with the burgers," said Anna.

Michael sighed. "I guess you are right. No sense in being so authentic that you leave out good food. I need to go to a grocery store early tomorrow morning. Where's the best one?"

"The best Italian store is Carafagna's Market not too far from here. The best fresh produce including meat and seafood is at the North Market near the Convention Center. It's not really a grocery store; it's a collection of individual vendors under one big roof. If we go early in the morning, the parking might not be too bad."

"Gosh, it's almost 1 o'clock. I think we had all better hit the sack," said Kate.

Anna was exhausted by this time. She took two more Advil tablets, put the heating pad between the sheets and climbed in. Pulling out her journal, she spent a few minutes jotting down her impressions of the day. Her journal was not a traditional diary but an opportunity to reflect on what was changing in her view of the world and what was not. This evening she wrote:

It never occurred to me that one could be an introvert and a type A warrior at the same time. I have spent the last 10 years complaining about too much volunteer activity since I retired. Yet I don't seem to be successful in putting limits on myself. My first explanation was that I am addicted to approval and therefore can't say no. I can't even refuse things that go against the introvert grain such as asking people for money during the church pledge drive, or knocking on doors on behalf of some candidate because the incumbent is a crook and needs to go. So here I am bringing in old friends from around the country if not around the world, planning an idiotic kid's game while dealing with an aging back and

unexpected bumps in the road. I feel like a juggler
who starts out with three balls and keeps adding one
every so often. I couldn't be happier.

She turned off the heating pad, put her journal back into
the drawer, removed Sumei from her pillow, and turned
out the light.

Short North Shopping

It was still raining lightly when Anna awoke. Climbing out of her pajamas, she pulled on a tee shirt and her favorite white cargo pants. The kitchen was already occupied. Michael was making coffee and had cleared enough space on the kitchen counter for a couple of bowls of cereal.

"Looks like Kate is going to sleep another hour," he said. "You want to go with me for groceries?"

"Sure. The house has already been cleaned. There's no point in getting out tableware until tomorrow. There may be a few people who come over tonight. I think some pizzas should be enough for tonight. Maybe a bowl of fruit and veggies plus dip. And some cookies.

"You have a final headcount?"

"Right now nineteen, including the three of us. There might be one or two more. The email from Beth was not enlightening. Who knows if she will reply to my questions."

"That's good enough to start with. You have a charcoal grill or gas?"

"Thanks for asking. I totally forgot about it when my back gave out. It's close to the end of summer so I probably should get another tank of propane. Can you get the tank off the grill and put it in the car? I certainly can't. Then we can go to the Short North. If you can't find everything you want there we can come back by way of Carafagna's, which has great Italian stuff."

"Sure." Michael went out to the patio, wrestled the tank off the grill, hefted it onto his mighty shoulders, and headed for the garage. He came back into the kitchen to get his grocery list. There he found Kate, still in her pajamas, pouring herself some coffee and checking her cell phone for messages. He planted a kiss on her forehead and said, "See you in a few. Stay out of trouble."

The Short North was a small commercial district on High Street, just South of Ohio State University. High Street was lined with top-notch restaurants, funky art galleries, small and large businesses. The next day would be the first Saturday of the month featuring the gallery hop at about 4 o'clock in the evening, filling the streets with thousands who come to enjoy the new gallery exhibitions, street performers, special events, food, and drinks throughout the district. The North Market was located about a block west of this district. Michael and Anna had arrived early enough to find a parking space in the market's parking lot, which was rapidly filling up. The building was essentially an indoor farmers' market, but one that operates seven days a week. Despite its inconvenient location, the market had a devoted following of people willing to pay extra for high quality food.

Michael was in his element. He interrogated each vendor about the source of the food, whether the meats were antibiotic free, whether pesticides had been used on the vegetables and other features whose importance was a mystery to Anna. She was relieved that he did not query the vendors about their political affiliations. It was close to noon when they loaded the purchases into the car and set off for home.

"Boy that surely is an interesting place," said Michael. "Where next?"

"We need to stop at Sears to get a new propane tank," Anna reminded him. She decided not to mention

Carafagna's. It looked like they had enough food for the party and the following week as well.

Arriving home, Anna wondered where they would put all the latest purchases. The kitchen counter and floor were already stacked with supplies.

"Don't worry," said Michael when he saw her alarmed expression. "Once I start cooking, half of what you see will become trash. In fact, let's bring in a large trash bag now. First I'm going to chop veggies for the crostini; then de-bone the salmon, mash it up and add seasonings and make them into patties for the grill. Glad I don't have to debone the hamburgers. I brought my own hamburger press. Oh shit, I forgot to get buns."

Anna gave him a notepad. "Here. Jot down anything you find missing and we will make a run to the grocery store tomorrow morning. I'm sure there will be other things we forgot. I need to check my email now. It looks like the sky is clearing up. Should be a fine day for the hunt and picnic tomorrow."

There were a few emails from those arriving Friday. Jean Chang, Dave Brunk, and the Magees confirmed that they would be able to join them for pizza that evening. Pat Soffit and entourage were going to a concert, but asked if 10:30 would be too late for them to join the party. Still no word from Beth Fowler.

Kate had been busy working on the clues and had an idea about how to start the hunt. "We are going to form teams of four or five, right? I don't think it would be a good idea for them to look for the same letterbox at the same time. So how about scrambling the order of the clues for each team. That way each team would start looking for a different box."

"Glad you caught that. It would be a mess to have a bunch of people arrive at the letterboxes at the same time. There still may be some traffic jams if some teams are quicker than others."

"Remember, the Conrads want to use their own car, so they probably should be put on the same team."

"Oh, right. That should not be hard to do. Now let's check the supplies and make sure we have enough table cloths, plates, napkins and weapons of mass consumption."

By 5 PM it looked as though some order had been established. They had three picnic tables on the patio, and the propane tank had been affixed to the grill. Anna printed out the list of clues for each team. Then she called Mama Mimi's to order a variety of pizzas which would be prepared for baking at home. On the way back home from Mama Mimi's, she stopped at a Kroger store to pick up the supplies Michael needed. She also bought a large fruit platter, chocolate chip cookies for dessert and a couple of bouquets of flowers for the tables.

"Game on!" she said.

The Invasion Begins

As Anna pulled into the driveway, she saw several cars parked at the curb. Toting the bags of groceries to the front door, she rang the doorbell with a spare index finger. Michael opened the door looking greatly relieved.

"Hope you have the pizzas," he said. "The oven is fired up."

"They are in the back seat, she replied. "Can you get them? I can handle the rest of this stuff."

Michael headed for the car as Anna made her way into the kitchen where she unloaded the supplies onto the large island, almost completely covered with Michael's half-finished creations. The Magees and Dave Brunk had arrived while she was away. Fragments of conversation drifted into the kitchen.

". . . Health Department is working on ways to reach the folks who are afraid to get immunizations."

"Yes, we had an outbreak of whooping cough last year . . ."

"George, I hear you are working on a new book . . . philosophy or ethics?"

"Believe it or not, I am trying my hand at fiction. Ethical dilemmas are at the heart of all detective novels."

Kate's voice broke through the din. "I have my hands full keeping Michael out of jail for trespassing with his protest signs."

"What is his latest crusade?"

"Right now it is a Board of Education full of science deniers. You know he teaches Biology at the high school level and he vows that he will not teach creationism along with evolution . . ."

". . . I've been tempted to write a murder mystery about someone tampering with dialysis machines by a zealot who thinks people with expensive chronic conditions should not use up scarce resources at the expense of healthier people. We had a case of such a sociopath at our hospital."

". . . Well, Dave, there have been many cases of unexpected deaths in hospitals later traced to nurses and anesthesiologists playing God . . ."

Anna entered the fray "George! Debbie! So good to see you again," she exclaimed while hugging them. "And Dave, you still have a full head of gorgeous hair. The gray streaks look pretty distinguished. How did you manage that?"

Dave kissed her on her forehead. "The secret of a long and beautiful life is to pick your parents very carefully."

The doorbell rang again. Dave opened the door and with a whoop pulled in a tall man in casual but elegant summer attire. "Carlos! I was hoping you would be here."

"How could I miss this opportunity," replied Carlos, his left hand on the elbow of an equally elegantly attired lady. "Let me introduce you to my wife, Peggy."

Anna and Kate converged on the scene to welcome the couple and usher them toward the buffet. "We will have a light meal in a bit. Do start on the appetizers and find a drink."

"This is such a great idea," said George. "I haven't seen some of the folks in 10 years. Who else is coming?"

Anna went through the list of guests then asked, "Have you two retired yet?"

Debbie laughed. "I have told him I don't want him rattling around the house whining about being bored, so he can't retire until he finds a hobby. As for me, I switched from hospital nursing to the City Department of Public Health. I love it. Working on preventive measures rather than on the ravages of years of neglect is so much more rewarding."

George protested. "I have hobbies. I write books. And I have to keep teaching because it keeps me in touch with all the things that are happening in a rapidly changing health care system. Have you read the articles in Time magazine by Stephen Brill about the outrageous ways hospitals find to gouge the public and insurance companies?"

"Yes, said Anna, "and it is a mystery to me why this kind of information did not get out to the public sooner." There was something different about Debbie. Her face was an older version of the younger and mischievous Debbie of a decade ago, yet age alone could not explain why Anna felt she was talking to an impersonator.

Michael snorted. "No mystery there. The hospitals and insurance companies have deep pockets which they have used effectively to buy legislators. Ever talk to any senators or reps? They have been programmed to avoid answering any questions directly and continue to spout the nonsense that competition and free market forces are all that is needed to bring costs down. There are no free markets in health care. There are just monopolies."

Debbie concurred, "There are certainly no free markets when you have to be hospitalized. Are you going to compare the costs or even quality of hospitals when in the middle of a heart attack or have just vomited up a quart of blood?"

As Debbie spoke, Anna found her answer. In repose, Debbie's face was almost symmetrical, but one dimple was missing. As soon as she spoke, only the right side of her lips moved. A closer look revealed a slight droop to her left eyelid. *Debbie's had Bell's Palsy since I have last seen her!*

Kate chimed in. "When I was hospitalized a few months ago, I was in no shape to ask the paramedic to take me to my hospital of choice, and since I was not in Knoxville, I wouldn't have known which one I preferred anyway. None of my network hospitals were available so the bill was higher than it would have been if I had gotten sick at home. Even if you go to a network hospital, you can end up with some higher than expected charges, say if the ER radiologist is on contract to the preferred hospital but is not on the "preferred provider" list.

"So, how is it possible to create an ethical system in the USA?" asked Anna as she helped Michael put toppings on the pizzas.

George opened another beer. "There are four principles guiding ethical patient care: Autonomy, Beneficence, Justice and Non-maleficence. Foremost is Autonomy. The decision-making process must be free of coercion or coaxing. In order for a patient to make a fully informed decision, she/he must understand all risks and benefits of the procedure and the likelihood of success."

Kate waved a hand dismissively. "Informed consent? What a crock! Ever been in an emergency room? Someone, usually a nurse, brings in a three-page form, and says something like: 'We need your signature on this form in order to do the surgery' . . . or whatever. Even if a responsible nurse asks a few questions to make sure the patient knows what has been proposed, many patients just sign saying that they can't understand all that gobbledygook and they are leaving it up to their doctor to do what is best for them. I have even had patients who were worried about a diagnosis of cancer say they don't want to know what is found at surgery. Just do what you have to do."

George nodded and proceeded with an indulgent smile. "As Kate says, sometimes a patient is in no condition to make an informed decision or even comprehend the diagnostic data on which a treatment is based. Another hurdle is that not every physician or nurse understands how to communicate this information, especially where language barriers and alternate cultures are issues. Beneficence is more complex. This requires that the interventions be provided with the intent of doing good for the patient involved, or for society in general. Placing primary focus on controlling costs, as hospitals and insurance companies feel obliged to do, often places this principle as a secondary consideration."

Michael glowered at an empty pizza box as if it had presented a consent form. "Of course beneficence is a secondary consideration. Any legislator who dares to suggest a public policy regulating profits is accused of being a communist at the next election cycle!"

He put the pizzas into the oven, slamming the door with enough force to dislodge a cup of pasta sauce precariously poised on the edge of the stove top. Anna, who was at the sink rinsing some dishes, reached out and managed to catch the cup, but some of the contents escaped, splashing onto her white cargo pants. She waved off Michael's apologies with a laugh.

"Michael, I fully understand the risks of standing next

to you when you are doing your magic in the kitchen. Consider this implied and informed consent."

"Well I insist on making reparations by buying you a new pair of pants. That stain will never wash out."

George resumed his lecture. "Reparations lead directly into the third principle: Justice. The health care provider must consider four main areas when evaluating Justice: fair distribution of scarce resources, competing needs, rights and obligations, and potential conflicts with established legislation."

Dave, who had been listening intently, found the opening he had been waiting for. "You may not know this, but nephrologists understood long ago that chronic kidney disease was going to place a great strain on resources, especially as the population aged. They persuaded Medicare to pay for dialysis in a totally different way . . . you might call it socialism."

"Really? Nephrologists are on salary?" asked Michael.

"No. For most services like consultations and treating acute conditions, they are paid like all other providers: a separate charge for each visit in the hospital or in the office. But when a patient is placed on long term dialysis, nephrologists bill for monthly supervision and may not bill that patient for additional services separately if they are related to the dialysis."

"Yes," Debbie interjected. "I worked in a dialysis center once. There were times when nephrologists did not even see the patient during that month. They could review the lab tests in their offices, confer with nurses by telephone and make any necessary adjustments without coming in. Now that is smart allocation of scarce resources."

"So, Professor," said Kate, "What about my experience with out-of-network hospitals and doctors who were not on my preferred provider list? Where does that fit into the ethical framework?"

"That would fall under 'Justice.' As we speak, Congress is fiddling with ways to change the way providers are paid. I am wary of an experiment to 'pay for performance' . . . meaning some providers will get a little extra money for good outcomes and others will be dinged for bad outcomes. So far as I know, no one is looking at eliminating the preferred provider provisions that have crept into the payment policies."

Carlos had found the beer cache and joined the discussion waving a Heineken. "All that pay-for-performance does is create another expensive bureaucracy to monitor billing practices. Clever providers are able to hire lawyers to figure out how to game the system. We should have a national health system like other countries."

"Amen," muttered Michael as he stuffed the pizza boxes into a trash bag.

Resuming his thread of thought, George went on. "Finally, ethicists look at Non-maleficence. All interventions have limited success rates. Side effects or complications may be worse than the disease. It is often difficult for doctors to successfully apply the do-no-harm principle."

There was a gloomy pause while all digested this discouraging information. Debbie appeared to be frowning, but it was hard to tell, as only one eyebrow moved. "It gets back to protecting profits instead of patients. But the trend in insurance companies, including the Medicare program, is to push for shorter stays and move some procedures from inpatient to outpatient status. This means they may not be psychologically prepared for the procedure, and in some cases may not be physically ready to return home on the same day as surgery. This is a pathway to a lot of harm."

Anna had finished scrubbing at the stains on her cargo pants and tossed the wash cloth into the sink with a resigned sigh. "And speaking of time constraints," she remarked, "there may be some physicians able to address the Justice components, but they often function in an environment where they are employees of a hospital or preferred providers under a managed care system. They are told how many minutes they may spend with a patient. And believe me, the business office keeps track of those numbers. I have friends who lost their jobs because they were not productive enough . . . meaning they did not meet their quota of patients per hour."

"So what do we do?" asked Michael. "Admit we are a capitalistic system whose main goal is preserving profits and say to hell with the patients' interests? Sounds like the do-no-harm principle applies only to the bottom line."

The oven timer began beeping signaling that the pizzas needed attention. Anna and Michael converged on the kitchen simultaneously almost colliding in front of the stove. The doorbell rang again. Dave, being nearest the door, opened it and cried out, "My God, it's Jeannie! We sure miss you at Miami Valley. How could you abandon us so heartlessly? And how come my hair has gray streaks while yours is a shade of red that defies description? Does that color have a name?"

"Got tired of shoveling snow in the winter, Dave. And I am gray too. I'll share my Henna Winetresses kit with you if you like. Hey, Kate, Anna. You are both looking great. Meet my friend Tanya."

With that all eyes turned to inspect a tall buxom African American woman standing next to Jean. The unspoken question in those eyes was: *what kind of friend?*

"Welcome, Tanya," said Anna, putting her arms around both women and ushering them into the living room. You came just in time for the pizza. Introduce yourselves while I get things set up on the buffet."

The conversation began to pick up. Seemingly, medical ethics was too heavy a topic for what was supposed to be a festive evening. They found refuge in talking about their families and other safer topics . . . for now anyway.

Kickoff

Early the next morning Anna and Kate conducted a post mortem on the pizza party over coffee and bagels. "I thought Pat and her ménage a trois were supposed to come here last night after the concert," said Kate.

"She called yesterday and said they had decided to tour the Short North which sounded more interesting than a concert and would join us before noon today to lend a hand. I told them the Gallery Hop was on Saturday, not Friday, but they said that was ok. They just wanted to window shop in funky stores."

"Any word from Beth yet?"

"No. I have given up on her."

"I had a chat with Carlos's wife and was surprised to learn she was from Syracuse NY. I thought Carlos was married to a childhood sweetheart from Nicaragua."

Anna leaned back to pick up the coffee pot and refill her cup. "That was his first wife. If you remember, he was captured by the Contras while he was in training in neurology. They kept him and other doctors in captivity for about a year. Very brutal conditions, but they needed the medical attention for their hoodlums who were injured in battle so they treated them a little better than other captives. Carlos and a buddy managed to escape and return to his home. Given that there was now a price on his head, he and his wife somehow managed to get across the border and seek asylum in the U.S. He had to repeat his neurology training because the U.S. does not recognize foreign credentials for licensure. Then two years into his neurology residency in Dayton, she was killed in an auto accident. He was nearly suicidal at the time."

"That must have happened after I left WSU. I'm glad he found Peggy. She is a classy lady."

Michael came in from the garage wheeling the cooler. "I'm going to get some ice for the beer and sodas. Need anything else Anna?"

"Not that I know of."

"What are you ladies up to now?"

Kate said, "We are going to check on the letterboxes as soon as businesses open. Why don't we pick up the ice and save you a trip?"

"No, thanks. I have some other errands to do."

"Well, be sure to be back by 10. Someone has to be here when folks start arriving."

"No problem."

The phone rang. It was Pat Soffit. They were driving up and down Henderson Road unable to find Concord Village Road. Anna laughed. "You can't always trust a GPS. Concord Village Rd does not connect to Henderson. Go back to Reed Rd, turn right and then right again on Mackenzie. It takes you right into Concord Village and Mackenzie merges into Montague."

A few minutes later a red SUV pulled up in front of the condo. Pat and Ted emerged accompanied by a middle-aged man with a gorgeous head of pure white hair. He was introduced as 'our good friend, Steven Duvault.'"

Pat handed Anna a large potted plant. "You said no birthday presents but I want you to have an orchid from my own greenhouse. There are care instructions taped to it. It is called a Christmas Star. There is a new spike forming now. It should bloom in December."

"Why thank you, Pat. I didn't know you had taken up a new hobby," said Anna, taking the pot and placing it on a kitchen counter.

Ted laughed. "You've heard of restless legs syndrome? Well Pat has restless hands syndrome. After a few attempts at helping me fix meals, I decided to build her a greenhouse in self-defense. It worked! Anything we can help with around here?"

"Nothing at the moment," said Anna glancing at Michael warily. "But since you are here, you can tend the house, answer the phone and redirect lost souls while we go out and finish some errands."

Michael looked worried. "Had any breakfast yet? I can fix an omelet. There are some bagels and cream cheese on the buffet, and plenty of coffee in the big pot." He didn't want Ted messing around with any of his carefully prepared food in the refrigerator.

"We already had the hotel complimentary breakfast, but the bagels sound good," said Pat.

"How was the Short North?" asked Anna.

Steven replied. "It was a hoot. They were getting ready for the Gallery Hop and some had their displays out in advance. There were even some strolling musicians. I had an interesting encounter with a mime who was engaging the spectators in a silent conversation . . . so I responded in kind a few times. Next thing you know we had a full-blown bit of improv street theater going. The audience loved it."

"Is the theater your trade?" asked Anna.

"Sort of. I have a degree in Theater Arts with focus on administration, but I participated in some minor small town productions. Nothing like Broadway or Hollywood. Now I mostly do radio or TV commercials."

"Your voice sounds familiar," said Kate. Do you do the voice-over for that ad for Omega Airlines . . . the one that shows a startled man having his coffee dumped in his lap when a tall man in front of him tilts his seat back? The line is 'Go with the airline with seats for real men. Go Omega.'"

Steven laughed. "No. Those are done by the big league players."

Ted returned waving a bagel. "Now if they would also build seats to accommodate the growing girth of Americans I would happily pay more for my ticket."

Anna picked up her tote bags full of the treasure hunt supplies.
"Sometime let me tell you about my long flight to Hawaii sitting next to a woman who spilled into my seat because she had to lift up the arm rests to be able to sit down. Come on, Kate. We need to get things organized out there."

With that, she, Michael and Kate left to complete their errands leaving the trio to tend the house. The two women started at the fire station, which Doug had confirmed could be used as one of their sites. Anna's phone rang as they were leaving. The call was from Beth Fowler, who wanted directions to the house.

"So you are coming after all," said Anna. "I gave up on you yesterday. Where are you?"

"We got back from Bermuda two days ago. Drove up to Columbus yesterday and stayed with Roger's daughter who lives here."

"Roger? Thought you were divorced."

"We were. Then we found out we got along quite well as long as we were not under the same roof for any length of time. He is a great traveling companion. Horrible as a housemate. He is an absolute pig. Never hangs up clothes.

92

Dirty dishes left wherever he last ate something. A trail of smelly socks all over the bedroom floor."

Anna could hear a voice in the background but could not catch what was said. "I think I hear a rebuttal," she said.

"Yes. He wants you to know that my chronic tardiness is a willful attempt to make his life miserable."

"Well, I don't think you are going to resolve the 'tidy vs tardy' dispute any time soon, but you do have plenty of time to get to the party and participate in festivities if you are already in Columbus." She gave Beth the directions, rang off and turned to Kate with a sigh. "Looks like Beth and Roger are back to 'friends with benefits'."

"They are both coming?" asked an astonished Kate.

"I'll tell you about it in the car." Then she and Kate retraced the route outlined in the clues, placing the last letterbox in a flower bed across from the Concord Village sign.

Arriving home, they saw three more cars parked near the driveway. Upon entering the kitchen they were greeted by Dave Brunk, the Conrads and the Wheelers. Eric Conrad was seated in the living room with a walker next to the easy chair. Sheilah, dressed in rope sandals, a blouse that could have been a maternity top, and an ankle-length pleated skirt, carried a large tote bag to the easy chair and set it down. Eric was talking to Joy Wheeler about his slow but steady progress in rehab.

"The diabetic neuropathy in my feet did slow me down a little. Affected my balance some, but I was able to get around without a cane if I was careful. Then I stubbed my toe on the sidewalk while wearing sandals, scraping off a lot of skin. The wound got infected and within a few days in spite of antibiotics the whole leg was swollen with red streaks heading for my groin."

Sheilah elaborated. "They called in a vascular surgeon who warned us that an amputation might be necessary. We were sweating bullets for a few more days. Then the antibiotics were changed when the culture and sensitivities were finally reported. He began to improve but had to have surgical debridement at one point. Of course he couldn't do any exercise for a couple of weeks, and by the time the infection was finally resolved his legs were so weak he couldn't even stand."

"That's not uncommon with gangrene," said Joy. "Even a few days in bed can lead to noticeable deconditioning. You can imagine the result when there is actual muscle destruction or debridement. I'm amazed that you can actually use a walker so soon."

"Was it one of those methicillin resistant staph infections?" asked Rob.

"No, it was a gram negative bacillus . . . pseudomonas. Unusual for a skin infection which is usually due to staph, so they had started with the wrong class of antibiotics."

"Maybe not," said Rob. "He may well have started out with something like a staph infection in the original wound, then developed a superimposed hospital acquired infection. Pseudomonas bugs are found everywhere, especially in hospitals. And they are very hard to treat. You are one lucky fellow, Eric."

There was a commotion at the front door, which opened to usher in Chuck Novak along with Jules and Sarah Filstein. No sooner had they been welcomed than Harvey Schulman entered, followed by Vivian Rogers. The living room was in chaos for the next thirty minutes as the assembled guests greeted each other and exchanged war stories from decades past. Kate made several attempts to get a head count, which was difficult as people kept moving around. She finally appealed to Anna.

"Is everyone here now? It's 1 o'clock, and we should get the hunt started before 2 PM if possible."

"Right now let's help people circulate. Put the sandwich platter out for those people who haven't had lunch yet. Has the beverage cooler been put out yet?"

"Yes. It's on the patio. Hope your neighbors don't mind all the cars along the street."

"Shouldn't be a problem as long no one parked in a driveway. When should we organize the teams?"

"How about fifteen minutes. Let's give them time to eat."

Meanwhile, the guests continued to get reacquainted. Chuck was interrogated by Sarah who expressed mock envy for his high-topped sneakers decorated with fringes that almost reached the floor. They were salmon colored, matching his short sleeved sport shirt.

"Wherever did you find those? My kids wanted to get something like that years ago, but I refused. They looked too dangerous for kids to run around in, but I really wanted to get some for myself."

"You can find anything online if you are persistent." He turned his attention to Jules. "Looks like your hair has slipped down to your chin since I last saw you."

Jules laughed. "Yes. Harvey and I are starting to look like Old Testament prophets now."

"Speaking of the old testament, I hear your son is now a famous rabbi," commented Harvey.

"Not just our son," said Sarah. "Our daughter Judith is a rabbi also. They have both spent a lot of time in Israel, but are now serving congregations in the U.S."

"You must be very proud of them," said Chuck.

"Indeed," said Jules. He paused, frowning, then continued. "We are proud of their commitment to a spiritual life and serving the community." His voice trailed off.

Sarah explained. "Politics can divide families. Seth is very committed to supporting the existence of Israel at all costs. Judith is also committed, but she has chosen to work with Jewish Voices for Peace, which believes the current policy toward Palestinians is going in the wrong direction."

"Ah," said Harvey. "Maimonides himself would throw up his hands in despair over that one."

Vivian rejoined the group with a plate of snacks. "Wasn't Maimonides a physician?

"Yes," said Jules. "He also found time to organize the rulings in the Talmud to make it easier to search."

"Imagine doing something like that without a computer," laughed Chuck, moving toward the piano. "Anna, is that electric music-maker plugged in?"

At 1:30, Anna tried unsuccessfully to get the attention of her guests, who were spread out from the kitchen to the outdoor patio. She was helped by Michael who did a two-finger earsplitting whistle.

"Time to bring your plates and glasses into the kitchen," he said.

Slowly the guests regrouped around the dining room table after depositing their tableware onto the kitchen counter.

"I am so pleased that all of you could make it today," said Anna. "I know you all want to get caught up with each other, but we can resume the conversations over the picnic supper that Michael will treat us to later this afternoon. Before that, Kate and I have prepared a challenge for you all to see if your analytical skills are still intact."

"I thought this was a birthday party," said Dave Brunk. "You are going to give us a quiz?"

"More like a puzzle." Anna held up a letterbox. "Kate and I have placed seven of these in the neighborhood. We are going to divide up into teams, give you a map of the area and a list of clues as to where you might find the boxes. When you do find one, open it and use the stamp inside to mark your list. Your list has my cell phone number in case those of you who are directionally challenged end up in the next county. The goal is to find as many boxes as you can before 4 PM when the treasure hunt is officially over. Please obey all traffic laws. I am paying for your hotel but not any parking or speeding tickets! Any questions?"

"Does the winner get a reward?" asked George.

"Of course, but that is a secret for the moment. Right now there are 18 contestants. Now, starting with Dave, I want you to count off from one to four to see who ends up with whom. Then you decide who will drive, who will navigate, and of course all of you need to consult with each other on what the clues mean."

After the counting was completed. Anna began to read off the teams: "OK. Team 1 is Eric and Sheilah, who want to drive their own van. They will be joined by Vivian Rogers and Steven Duvault. Eric will be the navigator."

"Great," said Eric. "Two family practitioners, a pathologist and a thespian. Since Sheilah will be driving, and I am navigating, that puts the onus of interpreting the clues on Vivian and Steven."

Pat interjected. "Sounds like a dream team. Forensic pathologists have to put together obscure clues, like poking around in stomach contents to figure out what was eaten, and figuring out from the angle of the wound where the assailant was standing. Steven should be good at word associations."

"Matter of fact, I am a genius at charades," said Steven.

Anna continued. "Team 2 is Chuck Novak, Pat Soffit, Tanya Lipscomb, Debbie Magee."

Pat spoke again. "Let's use my SUV. Never was good at charades. And I have a built in GPS in my car." She joined her team mates to pore over the list of clues.

Team 3 was announced as Rob Wheeler, Harvey Schulman, Sarah Filstein, George Magee, Dave Brunk. They decided to use Rob's car, which was the largest. Dave and Harvey got into an argument about who was the best navigator. Sarah settled it by observing that men were notorious for not seeking assistance when lost in traffic. As a middle-school teacher for years, she had learned how to deal with adolescent conflicts. She confiscated the map and informed her team this was non-negotiable.

As Anna was getting ready to announce Team 4, the doorbell rang. Kate opened the door to find Beth Fowler and Roger Comfort standing there. She was speechless for a moment. Beth was wearing a sleeveless T-shirt with a loud Hawaiian print, spandex black tights and platform shoes with four-inch heels and a maze of laces around her ankles. Roger, by now two inches shorter than his companion, held a small package.

"Oh, how great that you made it," said Kate, trying to sound enthusiastic while restraining an urge to strangle Beth. "Come in. We are just finishing lunch but there is plenty for you if you are hungry." She stepped aside and announced in a loud voice so Anna, who was near the patio, could hear. "Hey, guys, welcome Beth and Roger. We now have a psychotherapist and a pastoral counselor to minister to bruised egos after the hunt."

Anna winced. This was going to complicate the team structure. She came into the kitchen, gave the couple a perfunctory hug and said, "Glad you made it to Columbus after all." Roger handed her the package and said, "Happy Birthday, Anna. Hope you enjoy this."

Beth said, "What hunt?"

Anna thanked Roger for the package, which she put next to the door to the den, and led them into the dining area, gestured to the buffet and said, "We are about to send these folks on a treasure hunt around the neighborhood. When they are finished, we will have a picnic here on the patio. Have a snack to fortify yourselves and I will assign you to a team."

Debbie Magee greeted the couple affectionately. "I haven't seen you since we all helped start a hospice in Dayton. You look great."

Kate muttered to Anna, "She looks like a mid-life crisis to me. Sixty year-old women shouldn't wear spandex tights. And who wears shoes like that to a picnic?"

Beth circulated around the room greeting old friends while Roger, already endowed with a prominent paunch, loaded up a plate with potato salad, two sandwiches and several brownies. Meanwhile Anna retrieved her list of teams and reported the following names for Team 4: Ted Haney, Jules Filstein, Carlos Castillo and Peggy Mandeville. That accounted for eighteen people.

She said to the group, "Now that Beth and Roger have arrived, we can team them up with Jean Chang and take Harvey Schulman out of Team 4, creating a 5th team, totaling 20 people."

The next 10 minutes were consumed with clarification of places on the map and renegotiating roles. Anna reminded them that there was only one street leading into and out of Concord Village. They should begin the hunt by leaving the Village the way they had come in and not try to take one of the winding streets north to connect to Henderson as that was impossible. They were advised to seek the clues in the order listed on their sheets in order to avoid collisions.

"Avoid High Street," she emphasized. "I have it marked in bold letters. There is a football game at OSU and you don't want to be anywhere near campus this afternoon."

The team mates, having decided who was to drive, followed their drivers to the appropriate car; Sheilah Conrad leaving first, followed by Pat Soffit and her crew. Then Rob Wheeler ushered his team toward the door. Ted was elected to drive for Team 4, and Jean was chosen to drive for Team 5. As the teams began to depart, Dave Brunk broke away from Team 3, saying his car was parked precariously close to a fire hydrant and he needed to move it before they got started. He was very protective of his Porsche.

"Well, move it, man," said Rob. "We need to get going soon. I'm parked on the next street over."

"I'll meet you at your car," said Dave, hoping there were some parking spaces on that street. Dave's Porsche was parked on Montague Court facing the entrance to the Village. Rob was parked on a parallel street around the corner. Deciding to cut a few seconds off his driving time, Dave put the Porsche into reverse and roared backwards to the end of Montague, maneuvering the curve toward Sedgwick, planning to put it in forward at the next intersection so he could turn into the street where Rob was parked. Just after he managed to make the curve, his right rear fender clipped the front fender of a small Honda parked on the right side of the street, startling a woman who was mowing her lawn.

"Hey," she yelled at Dave, "That's my car you just hit!"

"Sorry, medical emergency," Dave shouted out the window. He tossed his wallet onto the lawn and said, "Here's my promise to return and settle with you in an hour or so. See Anna. She will vouch for me."

He put the car into forward and managed to find a place to park at the end of Sedgwick. The lady with the lawn mower, a short, petite blonde, cautiously picked up the wallet, and looked inside. *He really is a doctor,* she said to herself. *I wonder how he plans to drive around without a license.* She took the wallet inside the house.

Anna, Kate and Michael watched this debacle unfold with alarm. "What have I unleashed?" said Anna.

Baklava and Roses

Rob waited impatiently as his team got into his car. Teams 1, 4, and 5 had already departed. Sarah and George re-read the clues while Dave watched with amusement. "Where are we supposed to start?" he asked while Rob drove out of the village heading east on Mackenzie Drive.

"Station 2, it says here," said George. "The clue says:

Open Sesame won't unlock this door
Where 40 thieves have been before
When paying for your baklava
Request your mail from Samira."

Dave consulted the map, running his finger from one establishment to another. "Ah ha! There is a restaurant called Ali Baba on Bethel Road. That fits the 40 thieves reference. Isn't that a Middle Eastern chain? I know we went to one in Cleveland a few years back."

"Wait! Stop right here," George shouted.

Rob brought the car to a screeching halt. "What's the problem?" he asked.

"Look back there. There is a sign that says Concord Village."

"Well of course. We all know that is where Anna lives. Don't hold us up. We need to find Bethel Road."

George plucked the clue list out of Sarah's hand. "I know we are supposed to go in the order of the stations on our individual lists. But the closest letterbox is 50 feet from where we are. See here on clue number seven? *One if by land and two if by sea, and I at the opposite curb will be.* That is from the poem about Paul Revere's ride to Concord,

102

Massachusetts. The box has to be somewhere near the sign. Let's get it now and go to Bethel later."

Precious time was wasted as the contestants argued about the merits of this proposal and whether or not they should slavishly follow their instructions. George got out of the car saying, "Well, as your ethical coach, I must remind you that the fourth principle is Justice, and in the name of fair distribution of scarce resources, competing needs, rights and obligations, and potential conflicts with established legislation, I say that we are obliged to act efficiently and collect our stamp since we are so close to it."

He loped over to the sign. The others scrambled to follow him. It took them about two minutes of pawing through the adjacent shrubs and flowers on the opposite curb to find a box, open it and affix their first stamp onto their list.

"Woo hoo!" shouted Rob while the others clapped George on the back in triumph and gave him a thumbs-up for his masterful assessment of the situation.

"Now it's time to buy some dessert to celebrate," said Sarah. "Go to the end of Mackenzie and turn north on Reed Road which gets us to Bethel Road."

Meanwhile, Team 1 had solved the Smart phone clue, collected their stamp at the ATT store on the corner of Reed Road and were heading for their next destination to find the baklava. They arrived at the Ali Baba eatery at the same time as Rob and his crew were getting out of their car. Seven people (Eric remained in the car) converged at the dessert case at the same time, each trying to get the attention of the cashier.

"Wait a sec," said Sheilah. "We don't each have to get a baklava . . . just two of us. One for each team." She ordered a few pieces of baklava and while paying for it said to the cashier, "Would you please tell Samira we are here to pick up our mail?"

The cashier looked dubious, then said, "Okay, but I have to take care of some of the customers first."

Eventually the manager was contacted and arrived with the letterbox. Steven plucked out the stamp recorded their success on the list and returned the box to the manager with profuse thanks.

"Excuse me, ma'am," said Rob. "We are another team in this adventure. We also found this place on our own and are entitled to use the letterbox."

Steven smiled wickedly. "You are not entitled to anything until you buy some baklava, which you haven't. The clue is quite clear on that point."

He winked at the cashier, waved to the manager, and ushered his team out the door. There was now a line of customers waiting to pay their bills. Team 3 could do nothing until the cashier had finished. Rob ordered some baklava and again asked for the mail. By this time the cashier had caught on to the game. The letterbox was produced and the stamp affixed to Team 3's list.

"How many more of you shall we expect?" asked the manager.

"Three more teams are supposed to find you," said Rob, "But they may not be as smart as we are." They raced back to the car, piled in and started reading the next clue.

Meantime Team 2, chauffeured by Pat Soffit, had been delayed by a call from the surgeon who was covering her practice while she was on vacation. One of her patients, who was recovering from laparoscopic gallbladder surgery, was in the emergency room and there was some difficulty in finding her recent records. The on-call surgeon wanted to verify some information regarding her underlying medical conditions and any problems that may have occurred during the surgery. It took about 10 minutes and several additional phone calls before Pat was assured that she could resume her duties with the team. She started the car, raised a fist and shouted, "Onward into battle!"

The others were still arguing about their clue, which stated:

> I'm offered to the beloved, and also to the dead.
>
> I come in many lovely hues, most notably red.
>
> When handling me be careful, as some have bled.

Chuck noticed that a Park of Roses was located on the other side of the Olentangy River. He and Tanya were determined that they should drive there. Pat and Debbie were equally determined that the word "handling" indicated they should look for a florist shop.

"Look at the size of that park," said Debbie. "How can we find a letterbox in several acres of land that has hundreds of different rosebushes?"

"Well you have the same problem when buying roses," said Chuck. "They have flowers in every supermarket and there are plenty of those on the map."

After a heated discussion, a vote was taken favoring the Park of Roses 3:1. As they drove down Henderson Road to cross the river, Debbie said, "Oh my, the entrance to the park is from High street and Anna told us to avoid that street because of the football game at OSU."

Pat glanced at the GPS screen, saying to Chuck, "We can take Route 315 south to Broadway and get to the Park of Roses by going north on High Street. That would avoid the southbound campus traffic."

She maneuvered onto the entrance ramp for Route 315 and managed to insert the car into the slowly moving southbound traffic. "I think we are okay," she said. "We're going slow but the exit to Broadway is just a mile ahead." No sooner were the words out of her mouth that all the brake lights in three lanes of traffic lit up. She slammed on the brakes, narrowly missing a car that had squeezed into her lane from the left. They sat there for ten minutes wondering what had happened. Tanya muttered, "I hope they aren't playing Michigan; this could be the beginning of an epic brawl."

"Not likely," said Chuck. "That game is played in late November. But look what I found on the map! There is a store called Blooms To Go on old Henderson Road right next to Kenny. We just drove past it on the way down. I'll bet that's where we are supposed to go."

"Well, if we can just get to the Broadway exit, we can retrace our steps on Olentangy River Road and hope to get to the florist before dark," said Debbie. "I vote for going there first and do the Park only if we are wrong. But I don't think Anna would have sent us to the park while warning us to avoid High Street."

Finding her logic convincing, the others agreed. After another five minutes, they heard sirens and could see flashing lights ahead. Eventually an ambulance could be seen making its way toward an exit ramp. By 2:30 traffic was beginning to inch forward. As they approached the ramp they could see a battered pickup truck on the left shoulder and a small VW lying on its side in the median strip.

"None of those look like any of the vehicles I saw at Anna's," said Pat.

"Thank goodness!" said Debbie. "Otherwise we'd be obliged to go to the hospital also."

Chuck resumed his navigating job. "Turn right at the end of the ramp and head north toward Henderson. The White Cross Hospital is almost opposite the ramp. I can see it now. I'll bet that's where the ambulance went."

Traffic was much lighter when they reached Olentangy River Road, and they were able to find the florist shop quickly. Sure enough the letterbox was there. They bought a dozen roses for Anna. The next clue about baklava was quickly solved.

"Well, it's almost 3 o'clock," said Pat as they stamped the list. "I sure hope the remaining clues are less trouble than the first one."

"Amen," grumbled Tanya. "I think we should lodge a formal complaint about directing us specifically to roses instead of flowers in general."

"Go for it, Tanya," laughed Chuck. "Launch a class action suit and I will join it."

Cats and Collectors

While Pat and her group were stuck in the football game traffic, Team 4 had found Blooms To Go and left in search of the next clue which read:

> *We offer more than meets the eye,*
> *A home away from home and don't ask why.*
> *Too many babies? We have plans.*
> *Lump or cyst? Try our cat scans.*

"Sounds like a hospital," observed Peggy. They do all those services."

"But 'homes' doesn't fit," objected Ted.

"Sure it does," countered Carlos. "A hospital bed is your home until you get discharged. But I don't think Anna would send us to a hospital. Where would we ask about letterboxes? Hardly the emergency department. Admitting office? Parking attendant? Let's think of other options."

"There's an imaging center on Kenny and 5th Avenue," said Jules.

Ted laughed. "Since when do radiologists offer contraceptive services?"

Jules agreed. "And hardly a place to get lodging. But it's clearly a place for medical services. Maybe a nursing home? A hospice?"

"No," said Peggy. "No babies there either. It sounds like an orphanage, but then the scans don't make sense."

"A home away from home could be respite care, but then the other clues don't fit either," said Jules.

Ted tried again. "Pharmacies are now offering just about everything under the sun. They haven't offered overnight boarding yet, but I wouldn't be surprised if that turned up in their next business plan."

"I got it!" exclaimed Jules. "Animal clinics offer everything in that clue including boarding. Here's one called *Just Cats* on Dierker Road."

Carlos looked doubtful. "Small animal clinics don't have CT scanners. You would have to go to a vet school for that."

"Ah, but notice she spelled 'cat' with no capital letters, not C-A-T. So she didn't mean a CT scan. If you think a lump may be a cyst, you do an ultrasound, not a CT. An animal clinic could easily have ultrasound. Stay on Henderson, Ted. We'll get to Dierker in about a mile."

After turning on to Dierker Road, they saw a sign displaying a large image of a smiling cat that held a smaller sign with swirling letters spelling out *Just Cats*. They pulled into the parking lot and all four eagerly entered the large waiting room where they saw an array of small cages occupied by a collection of vexed and suspicious felines. Ted went up to the reception window where a cheerful red-headed receptionist greeted him before he could speak.

"Hi. You must be Anna's victims," she said.

"Indeed we are," said Ted smiling. "How could you tell?"

She laughed. "Four people and no cages? That's a no-brainer. Besides, Beth and Roger just left and almost took Garfield with them." She gestured toward a large orange cat reclining on a stack of catalogs behind her.

"He *is* gorgeous," said Peggy. "The mangled right ear makes him look rather debonair. Did they want to buy him?"

"Oh, he is not for sale. He is the official custodian of the office. Our customers would never forgive us if we gave him up. When I opened the window to give them the letterbox, Garfield jumped through and started purring and weaving around Roger's feet. Roger picked him up and they had quite a conversation before Beth dragged him away." She passed the letterbox through the open window. Garfield opened one eye, surveyed the team, and, evidently finding no chemistry in this group, went back to sleep.

"Rejected again," sighed Ted. "I'm going home and eat some worms."

The receptionist laughed, as did the waiting clients. An elderly man, holding a large cage in which a handsome Siamese was restlessly pacing around in circles, said, "I wish Tyson would be so humble. He can't wait for an opportunity to take out Garfield's other ear!"

"Garfield rejected him too?"

"Quite the opposite. A few months ago I brought him in because he wouldn't eat and was very listless. Dr. Kline had just inserted a thermometer into his butt when Garfield appeared from behind some boxes and leaped onto the table. Tyson went from limp to maniacal, lunged for him and the thermometer went flying to the floor. Fortunately it did not break inside him."

Jules chuckled. "Maybe we should send Roger back to give Tyson some anger management therapy." He extracted the stamp, recorded their success and passed the box back to the receptionist. "OK gang. Two down, five to go."

In the car, they consulted their list again. Their next stop was described as:

*I help you stay in touch with collectors, friends,
and foes
My most popular item gets put in a corner
and can go around the world
But never leaves the corner.
Although I have many boxes,
Yours will be outside where for $1.00
You can get caught up on the news.*

"Sounds like a place to buy furniture," said Ted.

"Or maybe an antique shop?" queried Peggy.

"The last two lines suggest a newspaper stand, but they can be anyplace. Usually in strip malls."

"Well," said Jules, "there are a ton of strip malls on Bethel but only a couple on Henderson which is right around the corner. Let's go there first."

Carlos consulted the map. He reported that there were a gazillion restaurants, two grocery stores, a thrift store, a couple of gas stations, a post office, and a Sears hardware store. "Let's go to the thrift store. I'm sure they have boxes and they do attract collectors."

Ted parked the car close to the thrift store. There was no newspaper stand by the door, nor next to an adjoining pizza parlor. As they walked aimlessly around the sidewalks, Jules commented, "Well I see a newspaper stand in front of that post office branch, but I can't make that fit the clue."

"Oh, I get it," cried Peggy. "It is the post office after all. The popular item is a stamp that you put in the corner of an envelope!"

They ran over to the newsstand, and sure enough, a letterbox was attached to one of its legs with a padlock. Fortunately the stamp was still inside. There was much whooping and back slapping as Jules stamped their list saying, "Three down!"

As they walked toward the car, Ted exclaimed, "Look! There is one of our teams."

Sure enough, Jean Chang, Beth Fowler, Roger Comfort and Harvey Schulman had just come out of the thrift store looking very dejected. Ted hailed them, greeting Roger, "Well if it isn't the cat-whisperer himself," he said chuckling. "Find any formal clothes for the party in there?"

Roger shook his head, while Jean said morosely, "We were doing fine up to now. We have collected three stamps but can't figure this clue out. Which one are you working on?"

Ted said smugly, "We just figured out what goes around the world without leaving its corner."

"That's the one we've been stuck on for half an hour," said Harvey. "Are you interested in a little data exchange?"

"Would that be ethical?" asked Carlos.

"Of course," said Beth. "The most civilized communities are those which collaborate for the common good."

"I think the team that returns first gets the grand prize," said Harvey." Right now, both of our teams are three of seven, right? If we help each other this one time, it doesn't put either of us at a disadvantage."

That sounded convincing to all. Team 5 was directed to the post office, and Team 4 was instructed to think about wireless phones.

"If there is a booby prize," said Jean, "I think Team 2 is going to get it. Tanya called me about 15 minutes ago. They got a late start and then were stuck on Route 315 in the football traffic. Apparently there was an accident just ahead of them but they finally managed to get off the highway."

"They're lucky they weren't part of that accident," commented Ted. "Thanks for the tip, Harvey. We'll see you at the party. Stay off 315!"

Where's the Fire?

While Team 5 moved on to the post office, Team 4 returned to their car and searched for the clue that suggested cell phones. They had only two clues left. The first showed a cartoon picture of a man talking into his shoe. The caption said *Get Smart . . . use the Cingularly best product*, while the other had a riddle about fighters.

"Isn't Cingular a wireless network?" asked Carlos. "But, I don't see a sign for Cingular around here."

"I have a vague memory of an old TV comedy featuring a detective called Maxwell Smart," said Jules. "He had a telephone embedded in his shoe which he used to make emergency calls. In fact I think the TV program was called 'Get Smart'."

"Oh yes," said Peggy, "I remember that show. There used to be a Cingular wireless network, but I don't see one on the map. Besides I don't think it exists anymore."

"You're right," said Ted. "About 10 years ago ATT and Cingular went through a series of buyouts and mergers, so I think the clue is directing us to the ATT store, and there is one at the next intersection across from the post office."

Encouraged by this information, they parked in front of the ATT store and went in. They were met by a smiling young lady, who by this time was familiar with the routine, so that when they inquired about a letterbox they were directed to the correct shrub.

"Wow! We are on a roll! What's the next clue? It's our last one so we might be the first team to return if we can get it done quickly!" exclaimed Ted as he stamped their card.

Peggy read the following riddle:

They call us fighters but we don't kill
Though we might toss you over the sill.
We break in your windows and smash down
your doors.
Saving lives is just one of our chores.

"Sounds rather violent," said Carlos. "Maybe National Guard or police? But of course they sometimes have to kill."

"That pretty well describes everything firefighters do," said Jules. "They have ambulances as well as fire trucks. Is there a fire station on the map?"

"Yes," said Peggy. "Turn south on Reed Road. It will be on our right side in a mile or two."

Meanwhile, preparations for a celebration were in full swing at the base camp on Montague Court. Michael was about to fire up the grill and was checking out the various items to be barbecued. Anna had just left to get a few more bags of ice for the cooler after instructing Kate to put place settings on the picnic tables on the patio.

Michael stepped back from the grill to mop his forehead and called to Kate. "I can't be in two places at once. When you get done with the tables, I need you to be in the kitchen to sauté some onions and mushrooms. I'm going to stay here and start pressing out the hamburgers and salmon burgers."

"Fine," said Kate as she moved into the kitchen. "What do you have in the oven?"

"I'm roasting some eggplant."

"Does it really need to be at 475°?"

"Yes. But it should be done in about 10 minutes."

Kate rummaged around in the refrigerator finally locating the sliced onions and mushrooms. She put a large skillet on the burner, added some olive oil and shortly thereafter stirred in the onions and mushrooms. She heard Michael call out to her.

"Kate, I can't find the salmon mix I made yesterday in this cooler. Can you check the refrigerator? I think I put it in a blue plastic tub."

Kate went back to the refrigerator, which was solidly packed with various cartons and containers. Eventually she located the desired blue tub, pulled it out, re-stacked the refrigerator, and carried the tub out to the patio.

"Thanks," said Michael once again wiping the perspiration from his forehead with his apron. "I didn't know Ohio could get this hot in September! I'll need to store the grilled items in the oven to keep them warm while we wait for the teams to come back. Anna figured they would start arriving by 3:30. But there are bound to be some stragglers."

Kate turned to go back into the kitchen just at the time when a shrill sound pierced their ears. Both ran toward the stove. Black clouds streamed out and over the counters: one from the skillet where the mushrooms and onions were now charred crisps, and the other from the oven. The fire alarm continued to shriek at top volume. As Michael entered the kitchen, a black ball of fur shot out of the den making for the master bedroom. Dodging the frightened cat, he lunged sideways, grabbed the kitchen counter with one hand, but slipped to one knee, striking his forehead on the edge of the counter.

Kate opened the front door to let out some smoke exclaiming, "Shit! I think she has a security system here. I don't know the code for turning off the fire alarm."

She ran to the hallway where the central thermostat was located and found the control panel for the security system nearby. The code was not written on the panel, but fortunately it had the 800 number for the security company on it. Meanwhile, Sumei found no respite from the noise in the bedroom, so he darted back toward the entrance hallway, zoomed past Kate and out the front door before she could grab him. She was dimly aware of a phone ringing, but decided to ignore it. If it was important, they would leave a message.

Michael rescued the eggplant from the oven and was relieved to find that the vegetables were fine, but that some of the breading had fallen to the bottom heating coils and had ignited.

Kate was in the process of dialing the 800 number when Anna ran in from the garage saying, "Where's the fire?"

"There's no fire," said Michael. "Just smoke from the stove. We don't know how to turn off the security system. What's the code?"

"Probably too late for that now. The company is supposed to call when they get the fire alert and we call to tell them to ignore it." She went to the control panel and tapped in the code.

"Well," said Kate as she put away her cell phone, "I heard the land line ringing, but I assumed it was one of the teams calling, and decided to use my time to call the 800 number so I didn't answer it." Then she turned to attend to the skillet disaster. "Oh Michael, there's blood all over your face! What happened?" She reached for a paper towel to mop his brow.

"I was trying to avoid squashing the damned cat and took a spill by the counter. I think I twisted my knee, too."

Anna and Kate inspected the cut by his right eyebrow. "Looks superficial," said Anna, "but you might have a shiner tomorrow. I don't think it needs stitches. Let me get a steri-strip to put over it."

"Speaking of the cat," said Kate, "did you see Sumei anywhere on the street when you drove in? He escaped out the front door just minutes ago.'

"No I didn't. But don't worry. All of the neighbors know who he is. I'm sure he will turn up shortly."

By this time, the alarm had stopped, but a new sound could be heard . . . the unmistakable sound of an emergency siren.

While this drama was unfolding, Team 4 had arrived at the fire station at about 3:35. Inside they found a group of men glued to the television set, watching the run-up to the OSU football game. Doug broke away from the group and greeted the team. "What can we do for you?"

"We're looking for the guys who smash in windows and kick down doors while saving lives," Ted replied.

"We can do that," said Doug with a laugh. "Which would you like today?"

"Don't need either right now. But if you know where we can find a letterbox, that would be just perfect."

"I thought you looked like some of Anna's victim's. You are the third group to come through here. Take a look over by that magazine rack."

While the team gleefully affixed the stamp to their card, they heard some urgent voices on the emergency alert system. Doug ran to the radio transmitter and picked up the call while the other men charged into the engine room and pulled on their boots and slickers. The team could hear only fragments of the message.

"You'll have to leave the building now," said Doug on his way to the engine room. "We've got to leave on an emergency call."

The team quickly exited, heading for their car. Within seconds the fire truck was on its way, sirens at full volume.

"Boy, talk about getting something done in the nick of time," said Ted. "Did you hear where they are going?"

"I didn't hear the number, but I'm pretty sure someone said Montague Court," said Carlos. "I sure hope it's not Anna's house."

"Well, we'll know in a few minutes," said Ted as he started the car. "We're finished and ready to head back to home base. If any more teams needs to get to this station, they will have trouble finishing up."

Upon consulting their map, they saw they were only a couple of miles from Anna's home. As they drove into Concord Village, they saw the fire truck parked in front of Anna's house. Several neighbors had gathered outside to see what was going on. There was no place left to park on Montague, so they wound around Concord Village Drive, finding a place to park on one of the intersecting streets and started to walk back to home base. Within a block, they were joined by Team 3, which had also parked on an adjoining street.

"What's going on?" asked Rob.

"Dunno," replied Ted. "We had just finished at the fire station when the crew had to leave on a fire call. Where did you just come from?"

"We did our last clue at the Just Cats clinic," said George. "We were on Mackenzie Drive and had to pull over when we heard the siren. Then we got to the Village and couldn't park in front of the house."

"I sure hope it is not something serious," said Sarah.

Dave said nothing, but privately offered up a silent prayer of thanks that he had moved his car earlier. Had he left it near the hydrant he would probably have had to pay a hefty fine. Fixing the little ding on the Honda was nothing by comparison.

As they approached Anna's house, they found the firemen leisurely returning to their engine.

"False alarm?" asked Carlos.

"Yeah," said Doug. "Happens all the time with these security companies. People can't remember their code, or are at the neighbors and don't hear the alarm. Well, it gives us practice anyway. And some extra income."

The two teams entered the house to find their hosts busily setting up for the picnic on the patio. Kate saw them first and waved them over.

"I'll bet you're thirsty. Come and get rehydrated. It's been a hot afternoon."

"Indeed it has," said Rob as he headed for the cooler. "Where do we turn in our stamped cards?"

"Just give them to me," said Anna. "I'll put them in a safe place for review later."

Kate laughed. "Anna has baskets that she calls 'Anna's Safe Place' in at least three rooms in her house. Then she can't remember which one has what she is looking for."

Sarah sank into a chair in a shady place on the patio. "Rob, if there is a Coke in the cooler, please get me one," she said with a sigh. "I have three safe places at home also.

The first is the wastebasket, which gets the junk mail right after I bring it into the house. The second is the drawer where I keep my check book and the bills and renewals that come in. The third is my desk, which at the moment is piled high with stuff I don't seem to be able to classify. You know, requests for donations to worthy causes, invitations to events or birthday parties, newsletters and so on."

Peggy joined her after pouring herself a glass of lemonade. "That last pile is awfully hard to prioritize, isn't it? It's pretty embarrassing to find I have failed to RSVP to an invitation and the event is already over."

Michael extracted the various gourmet burgers out of the cooler and placed them on the grill. "The first batch of real food should be ready in about ten minutes, but if you are hungry there are some appetizers in the living room."

Anna and Kate retired to the kitchen to confer about next steps.

"There are still three teams out in the field, and it is almost 4 o'clock. I'm getting worried," Anna fretted.

"Relax," advised Kate. "At least one has been delayed because Doug had to leave the fire station to come here. If there are any serious delays, someone will call us."

She then saw some familiar figures approaching the house. "See, we now have three teams accounted for. I can't wait to hear everyone's stories!"

Calling Dr. Heimlich

After collecting their stamp from the letterbox near the post office, Team 5 reviewed their last clue which started with the words: *One if by land and two by sea.*

"That's from the Paul Revere poem isn't it?" asked Harvey as they were getting seated in the car.

"Yes," said Jean. "I'm thinking horses, lanterns, ships. What else?"

"I don't see anything on the map that fits those images," replied Roger.

"Didn't he ride to Lexington to warn the residents that two lights in the church signified the British troops would come by the sea?" inquired Vivian. "I grew up in Massachusetts, and it seemed as if everyone in Middlesex County had memorized that poem."

"Maybe, but I don't see anything like a street or business named Lexington in this area."

"Any churches called 'Old North?'"

"Nope."

Beth chimed in. "When we called Anna for directions to her house, she mentioned that we should look for the Concord Village sign. I thought that Paul Revere rode to Concord."

Harvey whooped gleefully. "Yeaaah! Good thought, Beth. Revere did not go to Concord, but that's where the British were headed and a fierce battle was fought there. Let's head back to Anna's house."

The sleuths returned to Concord Village. Parking near the sign, they began exploring the nearby shrubbery for a letterbox, which they were able to find in a matter of minutes. While collecting their stamp, they saw a fire engine leaving the Village.

"I thought I heard a siren when we left the post office," said Jean. "Wonder what happened here."

"Let's hope Michael didn't send our picnic up in flames." said Roger, "I'm beginning to get hungry."

"Me too," said Harvey while privately thinking that Roger's heart would do well to experience a prolonged fast periodically. He had some difficulty finding a parking space near Anna's house. As they parked on a small street three blocks north of Montague Court, they saw Pat Soffit and her team walking toward them.

"Hi there," said Jean, "You made good time considering the late start and the traffic snafu you had to deal with."

"Indeed," replied Chuck. "Once we got past the roses hurdle, the Cat clue was pretty easy. Almost gave up on the one about collectors and corners, but we saw you driving away from the post office area and decided to look around there. Never did figure out the clue but we saw the newspaper stand, which fit the reference to 'news' and looked closer."

"That was a tough one all right," laughed Jean. "Not unlike the practice of medicine. You can't make the lab tests you ordered fit the signs and symptoms that are getting all the attention. Then a test you didn't order gets done by mistake providing a missing piece to the puzzle, and voilà, you are suddenly on the right path. "

"Yeah, but most mistakes aren't happy ones," said Chuck ruefully. "I remember my first month of internship when we had to start an IV on someone whose blood pressure had tanked. We had a hard time finding a vein because he was in shock. Finally went deeper into his arm and got blood in the syringe, so we quickly attached the tubing to the IV bottle. Then stood in amazement to see a bright red pulsating stream go backwards into the tubing and into the bottle. We had tapped an artery instead of a vein."

Harvey laughed. "Is that when you decided to go into Dermatology?"

"Damn right!"

On entering Anna's house Team 5 found their friends milling around the beer and wine coolers while Kate regaled the guests with the saga of the incinerated vegetables.

"Now you know why I don't do the cooking in our household," said Kate as she scraped the black crust from the skillet. "Multitasking is inadvisable for everyone; catastrophic for me."

"Kate, a reunion with you would not be complete without a dramatic misadventure," laughed Dave. "Anna, I need to run over to your neighbor's house and make amends. And retrieve my wallet."

"Her name is Courtney," said Anna. "Fortunately, she has a sense of humor. And a boyfriend, so don't stay too long. And while you are there, ask if she has seen a black cat. Sumei escaped when the fire alarm went off."

Michael came in from the patio, tongs in one hand, a beer in the other. "Everybody back now? It's after 4 o'clock."

"No," replied Anna. "Sheilah and Eric's team is still out. Hold off on grilling any more meat until they get here. Did any of you see them on the road?"

"Weren't they driving a big tan SUV?" asked Tanya. 'I thought I saw one with a handicap tag when we were on Kenny Road after leaving the imaging center."

"Imaging center?" asked Anna.

"That was our first interpretation of the cat scan clue. Maybe they got it wrong too."

"I'm sure they would call if they were in any trouble," said Anna. "Help yourselves to the hors d'oeuvres and tapas. We have some on the picnic table and also on the coffee table in the living room. And be sure to give me your validated clue lists."

Kate and Anna prowled the perimeter replenishing the appetizers as needed while their guests compared notes on their strategies.

"But that's cheating!" exclaimed George on learning of the exchange of clues at the post office between Teams 4 and 5.

"Hey George, " exclaimed Sarah, "You were the first to break the rules at the beginning of the hunt when you made us stop at the Concord Village sign."

A cacophony of mock outrage ensued. "What! The ethics professor cajoled his team into malfeasance?"

"Anna, do you have a copy of the ground rules? We have a serious breach of trust here."

"How are you going to pick the winning team?"

"How about giving points? There are seven letterboxes; 1 point for every attempt to locate each. Lowest score wins."

"Yeah, but add penalty points for cheating."

"Are some crimes more egregious than others?'

"I think we should form a tribunal for complaints against management," said Tanya. "Clue number 4 was clearly about flowers but the context of it pointed to roses, not all flowers. Did anyone else try to get to the Park of Roses?"

"We were on our way there," said Harvey, "until Beth remembered we were to avoid High Street."

Roger decided to add some shrimp to his already loaded plate, despite a warning glare from Beth. He hesitated, hand in midair.

"Relax, Beth," said Chuck. "Think of all the skinny vegetarian zealots getting older and older, trying hard to die of something. Better to die laughing."

That got a laugh from the group, especially Roger, who gave it an enthusiastic thumbs-up, then quickly popped a shrimp into his mouth and moved away from the buffet. Beth tried to smile but it looked more like a grimace. Most of the others did not know that Roger had already had a coronary by-pass operation. He had stopped smoking after that and had lost about 20 pounds. After their divorce, he had regained the 20 pounds and then some. She felt belittled by the comment. She was angry at Roger for lapsing, and also at herself for assuming the role of life-style warden. As the general conversation resumed, Roger continued to wave his arms, becoming progressively more agitated.

Debbie noticed that he was no longer laughing but appeared to be trying to cough. However, no sounds emanated from his mouth. "Roger, are you all right?" she asked, moving toward him.

"My God, he's turning blue!" said Harvey. Leaping to his feet, he positioned himself behind Roger and put his arms around his chest, placing his fist just below the breastbone. Roger slumped to his knees bringing Harvey down to the floor with him before Harvey could complete the Heimlich maneuver.

Beth began whimpering. "Do something for God's sake," she cried.

Pat Soffit ran to find Anna. "Give me the sharpest paring knife you have. Roger is choking and I may have to do a tracheotomy!"

Anna roused herself from a horrified catatonic state. Now that she had a task to perform, she moved quickly, located her purse and produced a Swiss Army knife. "Use this. It has a stronger blade. I think I have a bottle of alcohol in the bathroom."

"Shall I call 911?" asked Kate, pulling out her cell phone. She thought of having to face Doug for the second time in one day. *If there is a God*, she thought, *spare me that and I will start going to Mass again.*

Beth tried to stifle her wailing by biting down on her fist. Peggy put her arms around Beth's shoulders, gently pulling her toward the patio.

"Let's get out of their way," she said. "Pat and Harvey are very experienced in dealing with medical emergencies."

Beth moved with her, tottering on her four-inch heels, but could not tear her eyes away from the trio on the floor. Harvey had managed to get Roger into a seated position, but could not get his clenched hands properly positioned underneath Roger's rib cage, so he gave him a mighty thump between the shoulder blades instead. Roger did not respond. Pat cleaned off the blade of the knife with some rubbing alcohol that Anna had found. She knelt on the floor and scrutinized Roger's throat closely.

"Put him down on the floor and extend his head back as far as you can," she said quietly.

Instead, Harvey repeated the thump more forcefully. A rasping cough emanated from Roger's mouth followed immediately by the remains of a shrimp soaked in red cocktail sauce, which landed on Pat's T-shirt. Roger took in a deep breath, then lapsed into a fit of coughing. The color returned to his cheeks, and his eyes opened. He had no idea where he was, or why he was lying on the floor looking up at a circle of blurred faces, none of them recognizable. The first thing that came into focus was the shiny blade of a knife pointing at him.

Still gasping, he said in a hoarse whisper, "The wallet is yours. Just leave me the picture of my wife."

Harvey relaxed his hold on Roger and was quickly replaced by Beth who cradled his head crooning, "Oh baby, baby."

Kate put away her cell phone with a sigh of relief. Carlos gave Harvey a congratulatory pat on the shoulder, while Rob helped Pat get up from the floor. "Sure glad you came to the party. I could probably do a trach if I had to but it would not be pretty."

Pat moved over to the sink and scrubbed at the stains on her shirt. "Actually, I haven't done one in the last 10 years," she said. "Roger was lucky that the back blows worked. Usually, they do not."

Roger appeared to be recovering quickly. Carlos asked Beth to move aside so he could do a neurological evaluation, mainly checking his mental status.

"Should we take him to the emergency room?" asked Beth.

Carlos and Harvey concurred that there was no immediate danger, but that she should check his temperature periodically and seek medical attention if he developed a persistent cough or fever.

"There may be some small food fragments in his lungs," said Harvey. "Might result in a lung infection later on."

Roger got up from the floor and surveyed the guests who were somberly awaiting some signal that life could resume its normal pace. Anna in particular looked distraught. With a perfectly straight face and a twinkle in his eye Roger said as he bowed to her, "And for my second act, Anna, I will dive through a flaming hula hoop while balancing a glass of wine on my head."

Papers, Please

Team 1 had completed five of the seven puzzles by 3:30. They were stuck on the clue about cat scans. The majority voted to go to the imaging center despite Vivian's protestations that the reference to "babies" and "home" didn't fit. "I think you are reading this too literally," she said.

"Well, do you have a better suggestion?" asked Steven. "But it looks like there is a typo. Did you notice the way she spelled 'cat'? With no capital letters? If she meant imaging she would have spelled it 'CAT'."

"I've been studying the map for half an hour," said Eric. "I can't see anything else that comes close."

"Well then, let's go on to the imaging center." Said Steven.

Since no one had a better suggestion, they climbed back into the van and drove to the imaging center. There, the receptionist said she knew nothing about a letterbox.

"But," she said, "there was another group here about half an hour ago. They asked about the same thing."

"Well," said Steven, "I guess we are not the only dummies. Did they say where they were going next?"

"No, they didn't."

They went back to the van, puzzled and discouraged. "No luck?" asked Eric.

"No," said Sheilah. "Maybe we should just go onto the last clue and get that done. Perhaps one of us will get a brilliant idea by then." She smiled courteously at a man who was trimming the hedges on the edge of the parking lot.

Eric remarked, "I was chatting with that fellow while you were in there. He came here from somewhere in Africa as a refugee a few years ago. He was still chuckling about a lady who arrived just before we did. Very impressed by the 'beeooo-tiful black lady with nice bazooms.'"

"Well, there is a black lady on one of the teams," observed Vivian.

"Apparently she was in the office only a few minutes. He was delighted to get a second look at her voluptuous figure."

Steven looked up from the map and said, "Then we should find out if she came alone or with a group." He got out of the van and walked over to the hedge trimmer. They talked for a few minutes.

Steven returned with an elated grin on his face. "We're in luck folks. Our lascivious friend said there were three other people with her. I'm betting he was talking about Tanya, who is on Team 2, and fits the description."

"Does he know where they went?" asked Vivian.

"No, but he said there was a big argument about cats, so it has to be one of our teams."

Now Vivian took on the hedge trimmer. She queried him in great detail about what he had overheard, especially about the cats. "Do you think they were looking for a pet store?" she asked him.

"Na, na . . . just cats," he replied.

"What kind of cats were they talking about?"

The gardener waved his hands in helpless exasperation. "Day say, 'Just cats'. We go find just cats'. Den day get in car and go dat way." He gestured in the direction from which they had come.

Eric exploded into laughter. "Hey, come here and look at the map. *Just Cats* is right here and I never made the connection!"

The others crowded around him and looked where his finger was placed on the map: the *Just Cats Animal Clinic*.

"Let's go, gang," said Sheilah. "It's almost 4 o'clock and we still have one more riddle to unravel." She placed the car into reverse. The car was facing the imaging center, and there was a chain link fence behind her. They all heard a loud twanging noise as the car bumped into the fence. Sheilah glanced over her shoulder and decided to drive on as the fence looked intact. They made it to the animal clinic and collected their stamp with no further problems. The last clue was quickly unraveled as a fire station. They arrived there about 4:15, just as the engine returned to the station. Doug and his cohorts were busy putting their gear away and preparing their reports. Eventually Steven was able to get Doug's attention.

"Ah, the famous letterbox," he said. "Hope you haven't been waiting too long. We thought we would crash Anna's party before all the food was gone. Just got back."

"You're kidding, I hope," said Sheilah. "Was there a fire at her house?"

"More smoke than fire. They didn't know how to turn off the security control panel. You'll find the letterbox over by the magazine rack."

Having collected their last stamp, Team 1 returned to the van, and Sheilah pulled out onto Reed Rd to return to Concord Village. She had gone no more than two blocks when a patrol car with lights flashing came abreast of her and indicated she should pull over.

"Now what," grumbled Eric.

Sheilah rolled down her window as a trim young female officer, who looked to Sheilah as if she should be in high school instead of patrolling streets, approached. She greeted the officer with a polite smile. "What's wrong, officer?"

"You folks are from Florida, I see. Please show me your license and registration."

Sheilah got out her wallet while Eric got the registration papers out of the glove compartment.

"Here you are," said Sheilah. "I think we were within the speed limit for this street."

"No problem with the speed, but your license plate doesn't have a tag on it."

"That can't be. I put one on in July. You see the registration papers are in order."

"Yes, I see that, but the law requires you to have a current tag on the plate. I'll have to write you a ticket. I wouldn't advise driving all the way back to Florida without a tag."

Vivian got out of the car and inspected the license plate while the officer was writing a ticket. She returned with the news that there was a scratch on the back of the car near the license plate and indeed there was no registration tag on it. "I'll bet that when you backed into the fence a while back you left a souvenir on the fence," she told Sheilah.

The officer handed Sheilah the ticket saying, "You can pay online now."

"Does this mean I can't drive until they mail me a sticker from Florida?" she asked.

The officer shrugged, saying, "I guess you will have to call them to find out how to get one." She returned to her car and drove off.

"Boy, that was helpful," growled Eric. "She sounds like she is on the first shift of her career and eager to rack up points by issuing tickets. Let's go back to the imaging center and see if Vivian is right."

It was well past 4 o'clock when they arrived at the imaging center. After determining where they had originally parked, they walked back toward the fence and spent about five minutes inspecting the metal links. Steven was the first to spot a red fragment on one of the links of the fence. He carefully peeled it off and smoothed it out.

"There does appear to be a number on it," he said. "It looks like a seven."
Sheilah clapped her hands. "Bravo, Steven. That must be it. We renewed in July."

"Well," said Eric. "It won't do any good to try to put it back on. It is too small to pass for the real McCoy and we can't afford to lose it again. Let's just put it in the glove compartment with the registration and hope other traffic cops will accept the explanation."

Vivian agreed. "It's too late to call the Florida BMV now, and tomorrow is Sunday. Maybe you can get some useful information online tonight. Let's head back to Anna's and hope another zealous policeman is not on the road!"

It was almost 5 PM when they pulled into Concord Village, and, like their predecessors, drove around the winding streets until they found a parking place. As they walked toward the intersection to Montague Court, Steven noticed a black cat coming toward them. "That looks like

Anna's cat," he observed. He bent over and reached out his hand. "Here kitty, kitty, come to papa."

The cat stopped, eyed Steven suspiciously and scampered onto the stairs of an adjacent condo. Vivian laughed. "Careful, Steven. We've already had one encounter with law enforcement. Let's not have a neighbor report us for kitty-napping."

Sounds of merriment could be heard as they turned the corner and crossed the street. The door opened before they had a chance to ring the doorbell.

"Finally!" exclaimed Kate as she waved them in. "Anna is frantic. She was about to report missing persons to the police. Everyone else is here. Grab a plate and something to drink."

"We are already known to the Police Department," said Sheilah wryly as they entered the foyer. "Where do we put the history of our saga?" She waved the stamped clue card.

Anna ran up to greet them. "I'll take your card," she said. "We were really getting worried. Did you say you had a run-in with the police?"

"Indeed we did," replied Eric as he maneuvered his walker toward a recliner chair. "But it's a long story we can tell you about later."

Chuck was seated in the adjoining chair, and was just about finished with his beer. "I think we have a lot of stories to share," he said. "Anna, instead of picking the winner as the first to find all the letterboxes, I think we should hear everyone's stories and vote on which is least credible."

"Or perhaps which team made best use of scarce resources," said Sarah, winking at George McGee.

"Did you happen to see my cat while you were walking over here?" Anna asked Sheilah. "He escaped during our false fire alarm."

"Well, Steven thought he saw Sumei back at the intersection of Montague Court and Concord Village Drive, but the cat wouldn't come to him. Preferred the safety of the condo on the corner, so we decided he has a twin here in the Village."

"That was probably Sumei. He is the only Burmese in the Village. I'll check with the Sutherlands later and retrieve him. Glad to know he is nearby."

Michael looked in from the patio. "Hey gang, there are still a lot of burgers and brats out here. Come and get 'em."

Team 1 eagerly joined the repast, and the sharing of stories continued as Chuck moved to the piano and provided background music.

The Picnic

Vivian moved to the patio, picked up a plate and napkin from the picnic table, saying, "I'm starved."

"I'm thirsty," said Steven, making a beeline for the cooler and extracting a beer.

"Well finally!" said Michael, hands on hips. "We were about to send the police out to look for you."

Steven waved his hand airily as he walked back from the cooler. "No need to do that. They found us all by themselves and gave us a ticket as a souvenir."

"What! Sheilah the poster child for careful driving?" said Debbie. She turned to the others and said in a stage whisper "She's the only person I know who uses cruise control to stay under the posted speed limit."

Sheilah laughed as she sank into a deck chair. "I wasn't speeding. Somehow I managed to scrape the license renewal tag off the plate when I bumped into a chain-link fence. The newest graduate of the local Police Academy chalked up her first traffic violation."

That got a laugh from the rest of the group and led to a noisy recap of other traffic misadventures. Vivian, finding herself standing next to Tanya, asked with a sly smile, "I think your team also went to the image center just before we did."

"Yes we misinterpreted the clue about cat scans. How did you know we were there?"

"Did you notice the fellow doing the hedge trimming? Well, you have stolen his heart. He gave a very accurate description of you. And fortunately he was listening as he was ogling and heard you say something about 'just cats.' "

Tanya laughed. "Glad to be of help."

Michael returned to his post at the grill. He banged the tongs against the lid of the grill to get their attention. "Listen up for a minute," he said. "You have several choices for the entrée. For those who figure they have already lived long enough we have the supersized Bahama Mamas. Slightly lower down on the cholesterol spectrum we have the leanest beef hamburgers I could find. For those who don't eat red meat, there are salmon burgers stuffed with feta cheese. The vegans will have to do with tomatoes, cucumbers and corn along with the chips and salsa, desserts and booze. So give me your orders now. By the way, the kosher dishes are on the buffet with the appetizers."

Anna and Kate were busy bringing the side dishes to the picnic table as the guests clustered around the beverage cooler. Overhearing Ted say something about insurance fraud, Vivian joined the conversation in which he described the database of suspicious indicators of fraud and how investigators are using sophisticated methods to analyze burn patterns and determine the age of rust to estimate the age of damaged areas.

"Some claimants have tried to get repairs for damage which occurred long before the current accident. In many metropolitan areas, it's estimated that one in three claims contain fraudulent information," Ted informed them as he spread every condiment he could find onto his Bahama Mama.

Vivian spoke up. "Sounds like you have to practice automotive forensics," she said. "I work closely with our coroner's office. It's not unusual to find a presumed suicide turns out to be an artfully concealed homicide."

Tanya returned from the grill with a couple of salmon burgers sans buns. "I do environmental advocacy, not criminal law, but my colleagues tell me that false claims are a brisk business."

Kate arrived with a platter of tapas. "Tell me about it," she said. "I occasionally do medical review for a company that does Medicare and Medicaid claims processing in Tennessee. I'm ashamed to say that some of my colleagues have become very adept at billing questionable services for painful injuries. Some are from auto accidents. One anesthesiologist who specializes in pain management could use a rubber stamp for his history and physicals. All are very short and nearly identical. His standard treatment is trigger point injection under anesthesia! Can you believe it? General anesthesia for a few subcutaneous injections?"

"Yes," replied Ted. "We also get claims for injuries from auto accidents and find evidence of inflated charges, double billing for services, and even services that never took place."

Michael looked up from his post at the grill. "Maybe I should take a closer look at the bills from Kate's last hospitalizations. Wouldn't be surprised to see some padding there."

"Be careful what you ask for," laughed Ted. "If they send you the itemized bill it will take you a month to go through it and an army of lawyers to contest it."

Anna and Kate retreated to the living room happily surveying the group on the patio. "Had a few bumps in the road didn't we?" chuckled Kate.

Anna winced. "I wouldn't call Roger's near asphyxiation a bump in the road."

Kate nodded. "Right." Then she looked around the living room and kitchen. "Where is Dave? I don't see him on the patio, and he's not here either."

"Come to think of it, I haven't seen him come back from Courtney's house," said Anna.

"Well he is either having a really good time with your neighbor or she has assassinated him," said Kate.

"I doubt she has murder on her mind. It was really a minor dent."

Just then the front door opened and both Dave and Courtney walked in.

"About time," exclaimed Anna. "I was about to come over and see which one of you needed to be rescued. Come on out to the patio and get some food and drinks."

"I hope you don't mind my crashing the party," said Courtney, "but Dave insisted."

"Well one good crash deserves another," observed Kate. As the couple moved to the patio, she whispered to Anna, "I could swear she wasn't wearing those tight shorts when she was moving the lawn. I have seen that loopy adoring gaze in other women who meet Dave for the first time. And Dave looks pretty smug. Are we witnessing the makings of marriage number four?"

"I hope not. Courtney's boyfriend is rather possessive. As to marriage, Dave is caught in a cultural mismatch. He is not monogamous by nature. I've never understood why Margaret Mead was not taken seriously when she proposed that we should have several levels of non-binding marriages as people sorted out who they were and who they really are looking for," replied Anna.

"The hard core evangelicals will never let that happen," said Kate. "Just look at the flap every winter when they rant about the war on Christmas because some companies refuse to put reindeer and wreaths next to their logos. What do those have to do with the birth of Jesus anyway? They are pagan symbols."

Anna laughed. "Logic will get you nowhere when it comes to religious attitudes. People resist cultural changes of any kind. They fear a domino effect even if they don't know what the dominoes represent. And speaking of dominoes, we have another game to attend to. We need to get ready for choosing and announcing the winners. The original plan said the winning team would be the first to return. As I recall, Teams 3 and 4 were first to return and showed up at the same time."

"Yes. And then Teams 2 and 5 arrived after them at the same time. But there are some interesting alternatives suggested by our guests. Like giving points for accurate interpretations of clues and penalties for looking in the wrong places or for cheating."

"Maybe we should take Chuck's suggestion to award a prize to the team with the most entertaining story of their adventure."

"I like that idea. Let the victims decide."

The two women retrieved the desserts from the refrigerator and arrayed them on the buffet. Anna walked over to the patio.

"Ready for desserts? They are here on the buffet."

The Contestants Vote

By 7 o'clock, the guests were feeling pretty mellow. Some were still on the patio chatting. Others were arrayed in the living room either on the floor or on chairs and couches. Chuck had finished his jazz concert, and moved on to playing old familiar songs the guests requested and sang as he played. Carlos sang a solo: *"De Colores"* in Spanish, to the delight of the audience. Beatles' songs were favorites for group singing, "Hey Jude" had to be repeated. Tanya did a credible imitation of Whitney Houston singing "I Will Always Love You". This was followed by "Bridge over Troubled Waters", which left Carlos looking tearful. Roger was moved to retrieve his guitar from his car and give Chuck a reprieve by playing folk songs from the Vietnam protest era, immortalized by Bruce Springsteen, Pete Seeger and Billy Joel.

Happily listening to the singing, Michael and Anna took advantage of the interlude to start cleaning up, wrapping up the burgers, Bahama Mamas and corn to store in the refrigerator and freezer. As Kate had predicted, there was plenty of food left over. The beverage cooler, however, was in danger of being depleted. Michael wanted to make another run to the local Kroger, but Kate vetoed that.

"They do have to drive back to their hotels, after all. One police encounter is enough for today," she said. "I'll make some coffee instead."

Anna went over to the piano and asked Chuck to play a loud simulation of a drum roll to get everyone's attention. "OK, gang," she said. "Time to pick the winner. There has been a slight change in how the EMMI winner will be chosen. Since two returning teams arrived at the same time, that criterion cannot be used for selection. Management has decided that the contestants should do the choosing."

"Emmy awards?" asked Peggy. "We are going to select the team based on expert showmanship?"

"No," replied Anna. The award is E, M, M, I, which stands for Exemplary, Masterful, Manipulative and Imaginative. Each team will tell its story, presumably without exaggeration or fabrication, and you will vote for the winner. I will give each of you a card with the team numbers 1 through 5. Circle the number of the team whose story best fits the EMMI description. The team with the most votes wins. By the way, Management and the chef do not vote."

"There seems to be a contradiction in the criteria," observed George. "How can one be exemplary and manipulative at the same time?'

"And what about verification?" asked Tanya. "Teams are describing themselves. We need witnesses to corroborate the stories."

Roger nodded. "It's well known that witnesses are often unreliable. Their stories change over time and even when reporting shortly after an event that they claim to have seen, it is not what has been captured on camera. "

Joy agreed. "Perceptions can be misleading. That's why lab tests and imaging have become a gold standard. The word "pain" means different things to different people."

Harvey concurred, "I don't ask people if they have had chest pain if I am considering a heart attack as a diagnosis.

Some people vigorously deny having any pain. Especially women, who often do not report the classical symptoms of a heart attack as described in medical textbooks. It's better to ask an open-ended question about why they sought medical attention. Some report the classical crushing substernal pain while others something like, 'I didn't have any pain, just this awful pressure in my chest and throat, so I thought I had indigestion.'"

Despite Anna's attempts to proceed, the conversation degenerated into a vocabulary contest, wherein each specialist, in varying degrees of sobriety, offered alternatives.

"How about 'Efficient' instead of 'Exemplary'," offered Sarah, the most coherent guest.

"No," interjected Chuck. "I like 'Epidermal'."

"You would," laughed Rob. "So I will propose 'Epizootic'."

Steven joined the chaos. "How about 'Egregious'?"

"Ecumenical!" Roger shouted.

Other suggestions were Eccentric, Egalitarian, and, most confusing of all, Endopolyploidic.

Kate interrupted, laughing. "Hey guys, this is not a court of law. It's a game. Life is not perfect and neither is this way of picking a winner. Let's hear the stories, which should be a lot of fun. If someone is caught lying, the voter can decide to cross that team off the list. We all know voters don't bring logic to the polling place."

"Well, lying can be manipulative as well as imaginative," observed Chuck. "I see no reason why the lying team could not get a vote."

Michael entered the fray. "Indeed. Voting choices are usually made on irrational grounds, which is why sound bites and negative ads are so powerful."

Anna intervened. "We could talk all night about each one of these points, at the risk of alienating friendships. We are here to have fun, not obsess about rules. Team 1, let's hear from you first." She distributed the voting cards with team numbers on them to all the guests.

Eric, selected to report on their efforts, began in a pompous voice, "Our first clue was the Paul Revere poem and we spent a lot of time looking for a church that might match the description of the Old North Church. We were unable to find one in the area that had a bell tower where lanterns could be hung. Sheilah finally remembered seeing the Concord Village sign when she drove to Anna's house. We made better time on the second one about standing in a corner and going around the world. Steven figured that one out right away, so we made up a little of the lost time. The baklava clue was also straightforward, but our next one about the Cingularly Best whatever had us stumped for half an hour, as did the poem that suggested roses. We knew better than to go to the Park of Roses, but I think we hit every grocery store in the area looking at their flower section before someone saw "Blooms To Go" on the map. And you know the story of our trip to the imaging center, interrogating the hedge trimmer, and then getting a ticket on the way to the fire station. "

"I am impressed with your persistence in getting critical information from the hedge-trimmer," said Ted. "That's really *Masterful*."

"And how about that fluky encounter with the police officer? Maybe the *Imaginative* criterion should be changed to *Inadvertent*," said Sarah.

"You are free to apply the criteria as you see fit. Team 2, go for it," said Kate.

Chuck was elected to do the honors. "We got a late start because Pat had an emergency call from the doc covering her practice. Our first clue was the one starting with *I'm offered to the beloved and also to the dead.* Like many of you, we started off for the Park of Roses and got slowed down further by an accident on 315. This gave us time to reconsider our strategy and heed Anna's advice to avoid High Street, which is when we noticed the Blooms To Go store on the map. After that we quickly figured out that Ali Baba could provide the baklava. The next one was the cat scan clue and our first stop was the imaging center. Wrong choice of course, but I am proud to report that I was the first to spot the Just Cats clinic on the map. Our third clue was the Paul Revere poem. Debbie figured that out right away. Then we were stumped by the riddle about being in a corner and going around the world. We looked for antique shops, thrift stores, furniture stores with no luck of course. I have to confess that we gave up entirely the prospect of solving it, and went on to figure out 'firefighters' and 'Get Smart' rather quickly. So we licked our wounds and came home one stamp short."

Dave, whose competitive edge was in full force now, said "I think any team that didn't get all the stamps should be disqualified from the game."

There was a chorus of groans and boos. Someone called on George to mediate this suggestion, since he was the ethics expert. He started to say something about the principle of Justice having to do with honesty and fair-mindedness, but was interrupted by Jules, who observed, "Didn't we learn earlier that George was the first person to break the rules by leading his team to a letterbox not in the order mandated by their list? Who is he to be the judge of other teams?"

Peggy, who had been frowning as she listened to the revelations, said emphatically. "If the original rules applied, the winning team would be the one that returned first presumably with all the stamps. Now the rules have changed to have us vote on the cleverest stories. So why should getting all the stamps be a requirement?"

Jean agreed. "Hear, hear! Any list turned is valid. Let's move on to Team 3."

Rob began his account. "Well, as you are all aware, we were supposed to solve the baklava clue first, but George saw the Concord Village sign as we drove out of the Village, and persuaded us to get that stamp first, so blame him for the Manipulative strategy. We all agreed to go along with it. When we got to the Ali Baba restaurant, we found that Team 1 was there also. Steven managed to get his card stamped first, but refused to let us use our stamp until we purchased some baklava. That slowed us down because they had a backlog of customers to wait on before they could give us the letterbox."

"Sounds like Steven's team should get credit for Exemplary behavior," said Eric. "But then I am on the same team, so understandably biased."

"Hey, that's what good marketing is all about," said Ted. "Just look at political campaigns. Brag about yourself and insult your opponents."

Rob continued. "We didn't have any problem with the firefighters clue, but as with the other teams, we were initially stumped by the one which suggested roses. I thought we should try the floral section of grocery stores, but Sarah rightly said that it was unlikely that the letterbox would be in a high traffic area and we should look for florist shops. We found three on the map, and of course went to the wrong ones first before getting to Blooms To Go. But while we were at a florist shop on Dierker, Dave spotted the Just Cats small animal clinic and correctly linked it to the cat scan clue. So we went there out of order also. We did have some initial problem with the 'Get Smart' clue, but happily we have a team mate old enough to remember that old TV series. He shall be nameless."

"I proudly assert that I solved the clue," said George.

"Isn't that the second time this team went out of order?" inquired Steven. "Surely there should be a penalty for breaking rules."

"Or extra points for meeting the *Manipulative* criterion," retorted Dave.

The post office clue had us stumped for a while," continued Rob. The two doctors on the team failed miserably. Fortunately the teacher in our midst applied her critical thinking skills to the puzzle and reminded us that the reference to buying the news was a no-brainer and that we should stop obsessing about things in a corner and look for a newspaper stand."

"Cheers for Sarah," said a proud Jules, giving his wife a hug.

"Team 4 is next," declared Anna, ignoring Dave's attempt to skew the vote.

Peggy had been appointed to present their case. "Our first clue was the one about flowers, or more precisely, roses. Our analysis was similar to that of Team 3. We avoided the Park of Roses and the grocery stores and found Blooms To Go in short order. We almost went to the imaging center in pursuit of cat scans, but Jules noticed the spelling and capitalization used in the description. That led us to Just Cats without any unproductive side trips. There we learned that Team 5 had just left the premises after entertaining the clients at the clinic with Roger's encounter with the office mascot. Then we spun our intellectual wheels on the clue about collectors and corners for a while. Carlos directed us to a thrift store where we of course again had no luck. But then Ted focused on the last two lines of the clue and started looking for newsstands. That's how we got to the post office and figured out the meaning of the clue. Then we noticed the wireless phone store across the street, and solved another clue."

"Hold on there," declared Tanya. "I have heard that you didn't get to the ATT store without some help from another team. I think everyone should be apprised of the fact that there was collusion between Teams 4 and 5 at the post office!"

Ted laughed. "Well if *Manipulative* and *Masterful* are acceptable traits, I have no problem confessing that we found Team 5 floundering around at the post office after we had found the letterbox there. We simply did an exchange of mutually beneficial information in the interests of advancing the common good."

Peggy continued. "Our next two clues were the ones about fighters and the Paul Revere poem. The first one was easy to unravel, and Jules had trained in Boston so he figured out the Concord Village sign pretty quickly. We figured out the Ali Baba clue immediately and returned home. And do note that again a non-physician was the best analytical thinker."

"If you need some chemical assistance to see you through this challenge, the coffee is ready," interjected Kate. Several people moved to pick up an additional dessert and a cup of java.

"I guess we are up next," said Harvey, the designated reporter for Team 5. "Our first stop was at the fire station which Jean figured out fairly quickly. We were on our way to the imaging center when Roger saw the Just Cats clinic on the map and we figured out that the clue did not mean CT scans. As you have heard, Roger had to be dragged away from the clinic. We were stumped by the 'collectors and corners' clue like many others, but fortunately were walking near the post office when Ted spotted us and we had a mutually beneficial conversation."

That got laughter and cat calls from the other guests.

"Does that qualify as *Imaginative* or *Manipulative*?" asked Debbie.

"I can make a case for *Exemplary*," replied Vivian. "After all, many examples of progress in science are made from fortuitous observation. Alexander Fleming was a rather sloppy microbiologist who left some inadequately sterilized plates of agar gel on which he grew staphylococci near an open window. A mold appeared on the plates a few days later in addition to the colonies of staph. He noticed that in some areas there was a clear zone around the mold, which meant that the staph could not grow there. Thus was penicillin born."

"So one should take advantage of a fortuitous encounter even if it is dishonest?" queried Pat.

"The fortuitous element was the chance meeting of the two teams," said Tanya in her most lawyerly voice "The exchange of information about the clues was deliberate and premeditated. Clearly Manipulative."

Harvey got up to refill his cup of coffee. Returning to his seat he said, "We did not steal anything. We simply helped colleagues who were in distress. After that we worked on the Paul Revere poem, which took a while. We never thought about churches. We were side-tracked looking for stores that specialized in lanterns or lighting. After a fruitless trip to Sears and a hardware store we read it again. Jean thought of using her cell phone to Google 'one if by land and two if by sea.' That brought up a description of Longfellow's poem and the word 'Concord' was in the first paragraph. We found the sign and the stamp and went on to our next clue, the baklava, and quickly found the Ali Baba restaurant. The last challenge was the one about roses, and like just about everyone else we spent some time arguing about it. While we were standing in line to pay for the baklava, someone overheard us talking and told us if we were looking for flowers, Blooms To Go was the nearest place. We decided that was help sent from heaven and went there directly."

"How resourceful!" exclaimed Sheilah. "I call that *Imaginative*. Did anyone else use cell phones to investigate clues?"

Debbie shook her head. "Never thought to try. That's really a smart move."

"OK," said Kate. "Now it's time to vote. I'll give you about five minutes and then collect the cards.

And the Winner Is . . .

While Anna and Kate retired to the den to tally up the votes, the guests formed small clusters to continue earlier conversations and gossip about mutual friends. Roger and Beth were fascinated to hear about Peggy's research about the follies of the Catholic Church in the 15th and 16th centuries while Peggy was impressed with Roger's grasp of the history of Martin Luther's rebellion.

"You told me that you are currently writing a book about how the church in that era has relevance to the problems in Islam today," Roger began.

"Yes," said Peggy. "You probably know that in the 14th century, the papal court was located in the French City of Avignon and popes were selected by Kings of France. But when Pope Gregory died in 1378, rival factions sprang up. The Romans wanted an Italian Pope, and indeed the cardinals elected Urban VI, who wanted to reform the church, ridding it of debauchery and restoring the church to its mission of piety and salvation. The papacy moved to Rome."

"As I recall," replied Roger, cautiously eyeing a nearby plate of chocolate croissants, "the cardinals of that era were not priests, but princes and other secular individuals more interested in garnering wealth and power than saving souls."

"Indeed. Those eager to ascend to the papacy were hardly virtuous. To make a long story short, the cardinals, seeing their life-styles in peril, turned on Urban, declared his election invalid and set up a rival in Avignon again. By 1409 there were three claimants to the papacy, all refusing to abdicate. After much squabbling and maneuvering, the council of Pisa ended the schism in 1417. But the corruption and power grabbing continued under the Medici popes."

Beth was listening intently. "How does this relate to the current chaos in Islam?"

Peggy got up to get another cup of coffee and a croissant. "It all began with the death of the Prophet in 632. The tribal traditions of that era dictated that leadership passed from father to son. Muhammad had no surviving sons. Some of his followers, now called the Sunnis, wanted the community of Muslims to elect a successor. A smaller group, the Shia, believing in familial succession, favored Ali, who was married to Muhammad's daughter. The Sunnis prevailed, choosing a non-relative, Abu Bakr. At times these factions lived together in an uneasy peace, and at other times outright war."

"So your thesis is that all these conflicts are about power, not religion?" inquired Roger.

"My research convinced me that over the centuries, many of the conflicts we see come from failure of leaders, be they religious or secular, to act in the best interests of the people to whom they owe enlightened leadership and protection." She brushed some crumbs from her lap.

Roger got up, warily eyeing Beth, and helped himself to the coveted croissant. "That's what has fascinated me about Martin Luther. He tried valiantly to get the church fathers to reform. Even the laity had lost respect for the Roman church. He finally gave up and declared war on the papacy."

George had by this time caught wind of this conversation and decided to join it.

"Luther was in a favorable position. Unlike France, the German state was not unified in its support of Rome. And a larger portion of the population was now better educated because of the invention of the printing press. For the first time, ordinary people had access to affordable books. They became familiar with the Bible and the Greek classics. Humanist writings began to appear. The laity was already disgusted with the corruption in Rome, and embraced the rebellion."

Roger nodded. "Luther was able to get sanctuary despite Rome's attempt to assassinate him. The protestant reformation was launched and nothing could stop it."

Meanwhile another sober conversation centered on current politics. Michael was waxing eloquent on one of his favorite subjects, the war hawks in Congress. "Every time Darth Vader, AKA Dick Cheney, comes out of hiding, he asserts that every decision made in the Bush administration was fully justified. Yet he can't leave the United States because some of our allies threaten to arrest him for war crimes."

"I am quite familiar with US policy and meddling with regime changes," observed Carlos. "When I was in college in Nicaragua, the dictator, Somoza, was overthrown and the socialist leaning rebels, the Sandinistas came in to establish a fair distribution of resources to the oppressed population, most of which was living in abject poverty. Washington, apparently seeing this as a Communist threat, supported the Contras."

"I never did understand the dynamics of that conflict," said Debbie, dabbing at her left eye with a damp napkin.

"That's because our media ignored it until the arms deal with Iran hit the fan," said David. "Was it the Contras that kidnapped you, Carlos?"

"Yes. They needed medical services because their injured terrorist fighters were not welcome in the hospitals."

"How did they treat you?"

"Relatively well considering the field conditions and lack of medical supplies, which they had to steal. But sometimes when they were drunk, they liked to entertain themselves by holding pistols to our heads, telling us it was time to play Revolutionary Roulette. The rebels were a motley bunch of factions with varying political alliances, but mostly thugs for hire."

Michael's attention was caught by references to the papacy in the adjoining conversation, so he picked up his beer and joined them. Roger had just finished commenting that it took several centuries for the Holy See to acknowledge the findings of science and begin to root out corruption.

"The second Vatican Councils in the 1960s did a lot to recognize the legitimacy of other faith traditions and embrace diversity," Roger said as Michael approached.

Michael, who often described himself as a 'recovering Catholic' could not resist the urge to make his case against organized religion. "It seems to me that on balance, religious traditions have caused more evil than good. From Crusades, Inquisitions, demonizing women, conducting genocide or forced conversion, and justifying slavery, it's a mystery to me why this devotion to irrational concepts like God persist in enlightened countries."

Joy's interest in this conversation had also been piqued. She joined the group and commented, "Well, I was raised in a non-believing family of humanists. But as I worked with disabled patients, and became more aware of the extent of greed and corruption in our economic system, particularly in the for-profit health care system, I struggled to explain what I was seeing in humanist terms. It seemed to me that the rationalists in our communities weren't solving any problems either. When Rob said he wanted to do a tour of duty in the Ebola-ravaged countries in Africa, I started reading more about that epidemic. And one night I had what you might call a conversion experience. It didn't qualify as a 'born-again Christian' experience, because I never had been a Christian. You might say that reading *Ecclesiastes* that night made me a first-time Christian. The verses that spoke to me were: *a time to kill and a time to heal; a time to tear down and a time to build.* I knew then it was my time to do some healing in a part of the world we in the West had neglected."

"Not just neglected," observed Michael, "but actively exploited. We built an entire economy in the south on slavery. And then we sent missionaries to Africa. While they believed they were saving souls, they actually enabled colonialism, which left the countries without the skills to govern after their masters left."

"So you both went to Africa together?" asked Roger.

"Yes," replied Joy. "It seemed to us that the colonization of Africa by Western nations was the root cause of the chaos and poverty we see there today. Wealthy countries should not just stand by and let these crises escalate. We applied to Doctors Without Borders and were accepted. Rob's specialty in infectious diseases helped, I think."

Michael, initially taking Joy's testimonial to Christianity as a reprimand, found it hard to maintain his belligerent position when he saw the warmth and kindness in her eyes. He went up to her and said, "I have no right to malign your spiritual beliefs. I just meant that organized religion is often co-opted to serve secular and mendacious purposes."

She smiled. "No argument there. I still do not know who or what God is. All I know is that I felt a summons from some force outside myself."

At this point, Anna and Kate emerged waving a list. "Hear ye, hear ye, all subjects. We are about to declare a winner!"

Eager faces turned toward the buffet where Anna and Kate were standing.

Kate said, "We actually have a tie. There are 20 contestants. Six votes were cast for Team 1. The voters felt that the Masterful investigative skills demonstrated at the imaging center, and again in solving the mystery of the missing license tag were sufficient evidence for superior talent. Six votes were also cast for Team 3 because they demonstrated both Manipulative and Imaginative skills. Four votes were cast for Team 4, with notes suggesting they were most adept at figuring out the Post Office Clue, which all agreed was the hardest one."

Anna now spoke, referencing her card. Teams 2 and 4 also got three votes each, and Team 5 got two votes."

Kate brought forward two tote bags. "Will the winning teams please step forward," she solemnly intoned.

Sheilah, Eric, Vivian, Steven, Rob, Sarah, George, and Dave moved to the buffet

"We decided it was impossible to give an award to a team unless it could be equally shared by all its members," said Anna as she took a collection of wine and champagne bottles out of the tote bags and placed them on the buffet. "Now you decide which one of you gets which bottle."

The winners stepped forward, congratulating each other and sorting out their choices from the prize collection.

"You really dodged a bullet by not taking the responsibility for choosing the winners," chuckled Jean.

"Hey, we are anything but suicidal," laughed Kate. "But it did take a lot of discussion before we realized that the victims were the logical ones to make that choice."

Courtney had been on the periphery of the group, slowly figuring out what this curiously arranged contest was all about. She went up to Anna and said, "I can't believe you were willing to put together such a complicated event."

"Well, it sort of evolved, and I did have my doubts at a few points. Kate is a wonderful ally. We sort of fed on each other's ideas. But it was worth seeing all these folks again. I'm sorry your car was a casualty."

Courtney laughed. "In retrospect, it was pretty funny to have a stranger toss his wallet on my lawn and take off. Dave told me to send the repair bill to him. I assume I can trust him."

"I think so," said Anna. "There's one loose thread. My cat escaped and with all the commotion going on here, it appears he is not interested in coming back. Last I heard he was seeking sanctuary at the Sutherland's."

"I'll take a walk outside and see if I can find him," said Courtney.

"That would be great," said Anna feeling relieved.

Sheilah came up, giving Anna a hug. "Eric is getting tired, so we will leave now. Thank you so much for doing this."

Anna laughed. "I can't believe you are thanking me for getting a traffic ticket."

Sheilah smiled with a wry expression. "In the grand scheme of things, that is pretty small. Getting to see old friends is a treasure I will remember for a long time." She and Eric made their way to the door, carrying their prize with them.

Over the next half hour, the guests gradually began to depart after exchanging addresses, email addresses and promises to stay in touch. By midnight the condo was down to the three conspirators who were seated on the couch with their feet on the cocktail table.

Anna sighed. "I can never thank you enough for all you did to help with this orgy."

Kate rubbed her arthritic feet and grimaced. "I consider it material for my autobiography which I will write some day."

Michael laughed. "You keep saying that, but you are too busy talking to take up a pencil and write down your adventures."

Kate gave him a playful poke in the ribs. "Hey, that's who I am. A talker. When I am through talking I will write."

"That goes along with what Joy said about Ecclesiastes 'There is a time and place for everything under the sun.' So when is your time to write?"

"Maybe never. Here's a line for my epitaph: 'She finally shut up'."

Michael looked at her affectionately. "May that be far into the future. Anna, has Damncat showed up yet?

"No. Courtney said she would check with some of the neighbors, but I haven't heard from her. Maybe I should go out and look around."

Kate had moved to the patio with a plastic bag, picking up the trash. "You might start looking here, Anna. I think the wayward son has returned."

Anna ran to the patio where she found Sumei plaintively begging to come in. She picked him up, saying, "You poor thing. That alarm must have scared the bejesus out of you." She scratched his belly. "How about some canned fish?" She put him down on the kitchen floor and opened a can of cat treats.

Half an hour later, the exhausted trio headed for their respective bedrooms. Anna pulled out her journal and wrote a lengthy report on the eventful day. As she re-read her entry, she realized she had written mainly about all the things that had gone wrong or caused distress. It was full of self-recriminations for poor planning or lack of foresight despite the carefully constructed Gantt chart.

How careless it was not to put the security code in plain sight. And the clue about flowers should not have been so obviously for roses.

The litany of mea culpas continued for a full page. She closed her eyes and leaned back against the pillow, displacing Sumei, who then curled up next to her left hip and resumed purring. It occurred to her that she had for several days neglected a nighttime ritual established when she had the grandchildren with her for an overnight.

What good things happened today? Well, the picnic was fabulous, Courtney seems to have forgiven Dave, Sumei is back home intact, it looks as if Beth and Roger have reconciled, and everyone had a great time getting re-acquainted.

She added these observations to her journal. Then moved to the second question of the ritual:

What am I grateful for today? The answer is obvious. I have the best friends in the world: Kate and Michael.

She closed the journal, turned out the light, and was asleep within a matter of minutes.

Mopping Up

Michael woke a little after dawn. He rolled out of bed, careful not to disturb Kate. Glancing out of the window, he was pleased to see a clear sky, perfect for the long drive to Knoxville. Padding barefoot into the kitchen, he plugged in the coffee maker, then filled it with water and added a generous amount of Anna's Fair Trade Breakfast Blend into the basket. Returning to the bedroom, he changed into a T shirt. This one warned its viewers: *Don't Pray in My School; I Won't Think in Your Church.* He stuffed his cell phone into a pocket of his baggy cargo pants and finished packing his suitcase. As he sat on the bed to put on his athletic running shoes, he glanced at Kate who was murmuring something incoherent.

"Awake, Babe?"

Kate sat up, pulled the CPAP mask off her face and turned off the machine.

"Barely. What time do you plan to leave?"

"By 9:00, if possible. How about you?"

"I doubt if I can get organized before 10," she said, gazing around the room where her clothes and personal articles were draped over chairs, the dresser, an end table and various door knobs.

"Well that should get you home by 5:00."

"More like 6:00. I have to go to Mass before I leave."

Michael paused in the process of putting his shaving kit into the suitcase, visibly astonished. "Mass? You aren't even Catholic."

"No, but I used to go with you sometimes before you finally admitted you were an atheist."

"You were an atheist before I was. So why go now?"

"I promised God I would go to Mass if I didn't have to call the medics at the fire station to make another run here to rescue Roger."

Michael was about to say something about the I.Q. of people who perpetuate the notion of divine intervention when Kate interrupted. "A promise is a promise regardless of to whom or to what it is made." She stood up and began gathering her scattered clothes and folding them on the bed.

Michael gazed fondly at her, once again reminded of why he had fallen in love with her so many years ago. He decided this little argument was not worth pursuing. "OK. I get it. Let's have breakfast."

In the kitchen, they found Anna setting out croissants, bagels, jam, cream cheese and the remnants of the kosher kugel casserole Michael had made for Sarah Filstein.

"Anyone up for leftover burgers or Bahama Mammas?"

"In the morning?" asked Kate reaching for a chocolate croissant. "Breakfast should be high carb. It's the law."

Sumei, who had followed Anna into the kitchen, leaped up onto the island counter and sat down just behind the faucet looking expectantly at Michael, who was extracting his special cookware from the dishwasher. He packed his cookware and spices into a rolling cart and pulled it over to the garage door next to his suitcase. Sumei took a swipe at a small tub of margarine with his paw, sending it into the sink. Michael walked back to the dishwasher area just as Sumei sent a half-eaten apple after the margarine tub.

"Shoo," said Michael waving his hand at the troublesome cat. Instead, Sumei raised his paw again, aiming at a stray wine goblet that had not made it into the dishwasher the night before. Michael lunged forward scooping up the cat before it could complete the forward stroke.

"Anna, come get Damncat out before he destroys everything on this counter!" He dumped the cat unceremoniously onto the floor.

Anna had just returned from the den where she had retrieved a book promised to Kate. She laughed. "He just wants a drink of water from the faucet and is annoyed at you for ignoring him."

"But there's a bowl of water for him in the guest bathroom."

"Yes, but he prefers to drink from the tap if anyone is around to serve him." She picked Sumei up, put him back on the counter and turned on the tap, watching as he daintily lapped at the stream, then jumped down and retreated to the den closet.

Michael shook his head. "I'll be damned. I had a cat once who liked to drink out of the toilet, but never saw one addicted to faucets." He refilled his coffee cup and rejoined the two women at the breakfast table.

Kate sighed. "It was good to see Rob again. He was so helpful to me in getting a handle on getting along with the townies."

This was a term the academic physicians used to refer to the voluntary faculty who were in full-time private practice in the community, and a vital part of the teaching program for medical students and residents. Friction was common in academic communities between the 'townies' and the full time faculty known as the 'gownies.' The former viewed the academic physicians as having a soft job and not up to the rigors of real clinical practice. Unfortunately, some of the gownies viewed the townies as not quite their intellectual equals.

"What prompted him to volunteer to go to Africa?" asked Anna.

"He met a colleague at an infectious diseases conference who had recently done a tour of duty with Doctors Without Borders, and began reading about their work. He was so impressed that, when he retired last year, he and Joy signed up for a three-month stint in Sierra Leone. They loved it. I wouldn't be surprised if they went back again."

"That's not a job for the faint of heart, which describes me well," replied Anna. "Not only are the living conditions pretty primitive, there are still local conflicts where one may get caught in the crossfire."

"Indeed. In fact an operation in Somalia had to be shut down a few years ago because some of the volunteers were killed by terrorists."

Michael asked, "In addition to the indigenous violence, what's the risk of getting the Ebola virus yourself?"

"They have a very good track record. Few volunteers get the infection. They get intense training on sanitary precautions to protect themselves. The infection itself is less of a problem than the dehydration from the vomiting and diarrhea. And since most of those villages have no means of sanitary handling of human waste, or safe drinking water, the main treatment is isolation, cleansing, and replacement of fluids, either by I.V. or oral solutions, once the people can keep them down. An unexpected problem was the mistrust of western foreigners by the local residents. The Ebola medical personnel are dressed in hazmat suits when working in the hospital, looking like invaders from outer space, so it took time to get their acceptance and cooperation to work as a team."

Michael treated himself to another bagel. "Well, given Kate's propensity for inviting chaos, I'm sure glad she never felt the call."

Kate reached for another croissant. "Are you saying you didn't enjoy this weekend?"

"It was special," replied Michael with a straight face. "Just promise me no more joint adventures for at least six months. I need to recuperate."

Anna chuckled. "I see you didn't get a shiner after all. Hope that cut over your eye doesn't leave you with a scar."

Kate peeled off the Band-Aid that had been placed over his eyebrow and inspected the wound. "I think it will be barely visible in a few weeks."

"Well, I need to shove off," he said as he took his cup and plate and placed them in the sink. "I'll leave you two to clean up the remnants of the party. If I have missed anything I should take back, just put it in Kate's car." He gave Anna a hug and kissed Kate. Then he moved his suitcase and supply boxes into the garage. Kate went with him to help load the car, while Anna loaded the dishwasher with another load of dirty dishes and glasses.

When Kate returned, Anna said to her, "I'm glad I got a few minutes to chat with Jean Chang. Before I got my specialty certification in Rheumatology, she and I used to supervise the outpatient clinics in two of the hospitals affiliated with the medical school. She was an outstanding clinician. Some of the outpatients had been coming there for years and had huge charts. If things didn't make sense, you could count on her to do a thorough review of the charts, which sometimes led to a better diagnosis or treatment plan."

Kate replied, "Yes, she was great. I remember the time when a patient with lupus was admitted with a relapse of pericarditis. The residents were so used to having her come in with relapses that they hardly examined her. Just admitted her and gave her a huge dose of IV prednisone, and were thinking of adding some chemo drugs as well. Jean was the attending physician for morning rounds that week, and annoyed the residents by taking 10 minutes to do a thorough review of symptoms and a detailed physical."

"Sounds like Jean," observed Anna. "I'll bet she picked up on things they missed."

"Indeed. The patient turned out to be six months pregnant, which means the residents had not examined her for at least three months."

"So the chemo drugs would have been contraindicated."

"Had they done their job properly, they might have recommended a therapeutic abortion early in the pregnancy. Sometimes pregnancy can exacerbate the disease."

"Well, as a reward for doing her job well," grumbled Anna, "the hospital administration called her in and told her she was taking too much time with the patients and should be more productive. I think that was partially responsible for her move to the southwest. She found a neighborhood health center that prided itself on holistic care."

"Is that where she met Tanya?" asked Kate.

"No, they met at a Sierra Club hiking vacation in the Rocky Mountains. I think it was one of those vacations where you participate in some ecologically sound service project."

"Any romance there?"

"I didn't ask, but I got the sense that they just have common interests in the environment and other activities. And, like you and me, they schedule vacations together."

Kate got up, loaded her tableware into the dishwasher and said, "I guess I need to clean up the environment in my bedroom and pack up my car also."

Half an hour later, the two loaded Kate's baggage into her car and exchanged fond goodbyes. Kate opened the driver's side door and then stopped.

"Anna, isn't that Dave's Porsche over there?" She pointed toward Courtney's house.

Anna stared, astounded. "I think you are right."

They looked at each other, eyebrows raised skyward.

"None of my business," said Anna, giving Kate a hug.

"Nor mine," said Kate. "But if you learn anything interesting, be sure to tell me."

Dave

Dave Brunk had left the party around 11:00 to return to his hotel. He decided to spend another night in the hotel rather than drive back to Dayton, having imbibed a fair amount of wine. As he was moving his garment bag from the trunk to the back of his car, he noticed Courtney coming toward him.

"Hi there," he said, "What keeps you up so late?"

"I told Anna I would look around the block and see if I could capture Sumei. He escaped during the fire alarm debacle."

"Any luck?"

"No. I just sent Anna a text that I couldn't find him."

There was an awkward pause while each contemplated what to say next without knowing exactly what they wanted to say. Dave spoke first.

"I want to say again I think you were very gracious about the accident."

"Don't give it another thought. I will send you the bill when I get it from the Honda service department."

"Did I give you my address?" he said, hoping he had not and would have an opportunity to extend the conversation.

"Yes you did," she replied, also searching for something else to say. She had really enjoyed his brief visit at which time he seemed so interested in her gardening projects that she had given him an extended tour of her perennial garden. A light bulb went off in her head. "My hostas are ready for division, and if you would like to take some back I can get a few ready for you in a jiffy."

Dave had moved into a rented condo six months ago while sorting out where he wanted to live after the divorce. *I have no place to put them,* he thought. *On the other hand, Carpe diem.* "Why yes, thank you," he said closing the door of his car and locking it. He walked back to her house with her, lightly touching her left elbow when she stepped over the curb onto the sidewalk.

"You must have lived here quite a while to get your yard looking so professional."

"Actually about five years, but I didn't have time to do anything the first three. Then I was fired after the recession and had more time on my hands than money, so I started doing a lot of things for myself," she said, opening the front door and stepping into the hall. "Come in. Would you like a cup of coffee?"

Dave didn't need any more coffee, but the invitation was encouraging so he said, "Just a glass of water, thanks."

They went into the kitchen. Courtney filled two glasses with water. They sat down at the breakfast table, both still feeling clumsy and strangely shy. The telephone on the kitchen wall rang.

Courtney glanced at the ID, hesitated, then picked it up and without any greeting said quickly, "It's late, and I'm tired and I don't want to talk. I'll call you tomorrow." She hung up and unplugged the phone. She looked at Dave apologetically and said, "Sounded rude, didn't I?"

Dave, well experienced in relationships gone sour, felt his confidence returning. "Boyfriend problems?"

She nodded, not sure she wanted to say anything more, but he was so easy to talk to and there appeared to be no judgment in his demeanor.

"Yes." A long pause; then, "It's been a roller coaster for a couple of months, especially since I have been trying to get a job that paid a living wage. There haven't been any that paid above minimum wage. So I know I have been irritable a lot, and that has fueled a lot of arguments."

In medical school, Dave had been trained in the art of therapeutic interviewing, and the school of hard knocks had supplemented his skills. He simply said, "Arguments?" and waited for a reply.

Courtney shrugged her shoulders and said, "You know, he complains about something trivial and I say something dumb like, 'I wish that is all I had to think about,' and then he says, 'Well, if you had finished college maybe you could have held onto your job.' A few minutes later we are screaming and yelling at each other, after which he storms out of the house slamming the door, and calling me a bitch or worse."

To Dave, this brief description had all the earmarks of an abusive relationship, and from the framing of her responses, he was equally sure that she was blaming herself for the recurrent battles. He also knew, from watching the same dynamic in his parents' marriage, that it was hard for the abused partner to recognize the problem and deal with it effectively. He desperately wanted to know if she had ever been physically assaulted, but knew better than to ask. So, knowing that damaged self-esteem is the central weapon for the manipulations of the abuser, he just said, "You clearly are not dumb. You are hard-working and very creative."

She smiled at that and said, "Thanks. But I don't want to burden you with my personal problems. Let me just get the hostas for you so you can be on your way and get some sleep."

He waved her back into her seat. "In a minute. I'd like to know what your dream job would be like."

She immediately became animated. "Oh I have had several dreams. My last well paid job was in the HR department of one of the big banks in town. I was putting aside as much money as I could into savings, hoping to set up a Bed and Breakfast. Now I am depleting my savings while trying to pay down the mortgage on this house."

For the next fifteen minutes Dave listened as she described the research she had done on this particular kind of business and the contacts she had established in laying the foundation for realizing this dream. She seemed oblivious to the passage of time until she glanced at the clock and cried, "Oh my gosh! Look at the time! I have bent your ear about this and forgotten about the hostas. I'll get them right now."

Dave stood up and gently said, "I think you need to go to bed and get some rest before you decide what you are going to tell boyfriend tomorrow. How about I stop by in the morning on my way back to Dayton and pick up the hostas then?"

They were both secretly pleased about the possibility of another encounter. So she replied quickly. "OK. I really do need to get some sleep before I call Alan."

As they walked toward the front door, Dave's unease about her situation grew, yet he was aware that if he confronted her with his concerns, she would probably get defensive. He finally decided he would rather offend her than leave and learn later that something dreadful had happened. He paused by the door, hand on the knob, but turned to face her.

"Forgive me for speaking so bluntly, but I think I know what you are going through. My father sometimes vented his rage on the family, especially on my mother. By the time I finished high school I begged her to leave him, but she always found an excuse to stay with him because he was a pretty nice fellow between the rages."

Courtney was indeed shocked by his frankness. She moved away from him and folded her arms across her chest. Tossing her head back defiantly she said in clipped tones, "Alan does not have rages. I know that I can be provocative. He is a very sweet and loving person and is always the first to start a reconciliation."

The pattern of alternating abuse with sweet-talk, was familiar to Dave. He could see through her defensiveness, but knew it would be a long time before she could accept the reality of the situation. "I apologize for invading your private space. And I do want to come by again tomorrow."

He opened the door and glanced up and down the street to see if any cars were cruising by. Then he turned back and said, "But please, be sure to lock your door tonight."

He stepped out, got into his car and drove away. A short time later, he noticed a black SUV following him. At first he was alarmed, but then the car turned in the opposite direction when he reached Reed Road, and was not seen again.

The next morning, he got up at 7:00, dressed, and checked out. On the way back to Courtney's house, he stopped by a Panera and picked up some breakfast goodies. Parking in her driveway, he walked up to the door and rang the doorbell. There was no answer. After several more attempts, equally futile, he went around to the back of the house, made an educated guess as to which window was the bedroom window and rapped on it. Again there was no answer, so he returned to the front door and hammered on it loudly, wondering if he should call the police.

Then he heard a voice on the other side of the door. "David, I don't feel well. Thanks for coming by, but just go on home. I'm going back to bed."

Dave was pretty sure he knew why she wasn't feeling well, and equally sure he was not going to go home at this juncture. Not sure what approach would reach her, he decided to get right to the point.

"Alan came by last night didn't he? And that's why you are not feeling well."

A faint sob. "Just go home. I can deal with this myself."

"I am not moving from this doorstep until you open the door. And besides I brought breakfast."

The next few minutes were consumed with a repetition of his determination to stay and her pleas for him to leave. He was encouraged that she was willing to continue the conversation and finally pulled out the trump card.

"There's nothing you can say that I haven't heard before; nothing I will see that I haven't seen before. Right now don't think of me as a friend, but as a doctor, which I'm guessing you need. So open the door and let's talk about next steps."

There was a long pause. Then he heard the lock click back and the door opened. When he walked in, Courtney turned away quickly and walked to the kitchen. Knowing what he would see, he followed her, grasped her shoulders and turned her toward him. As he expected, her face was bruised, lips swollen and one eye blackened.

He stroked her hair and said, "Didn't lock the door?"

"He has a key."

"Ah. Should have realized that. Let's get some ice packs for the outside of you, and some hot coffee into you."

"I'm so ashamed."

Dave got out some plates and cups. "You realize that is what he intended you to feel, right?"

She looked puzzled.

More gently, he said, "And I hope you realize you are not safe anymore?"

"I have no place to go. No family here."

"I checked on the internet last night. There is a shelter house here in Columbus for women who are not safe at home."

"But . . ."

"Eat."

As she began to nibble on the egg sandwich, he collected some dish towels, dampened them in water and placed them in the freezer. "In half an hour, take one of these out, put it in a plastic bag and apply to your face."

She smiled gingerly. "You know, he never hit me before."

"There is a pattern of escalation before the hitting starts," he replied. "When you refused to talk to him last night, he sensed he was losing control over you, and that is the dangerous period. I think he drove by last night and saw my car and followed me for a few blocks. Black SUV?"

"Yes."

"Well, he is bound to come back, either to sweet talk you into another reconciliation, or to make threats. Might even stalk you. You need a plan."

She looked at him blankly, still unwilling to face the prospect that this relationship was beyond repair. After a long pause, Dave tried again, "Forgive me for butting in, but I have to leave for Dayton soon and I am afraid to leave you defenseless. For starters, get your locks changed tomorrow."

That sounded simple enough, so she nodded.

"Please call the police and get a restraining order," he added knowing this might be impossible for her to do. Sure enough she reacted sharply.

"Oh, no. I want to keep this as quiet as possible. I just got a new job as a temp secretary at an auto dealership. I probably will have to call in sick for a few days anyway, and I don't want police around the neighborhood or calling me at work."

"At least ask Anna if you can spend the night with her until you get the locks changed."

She grimaced. "I'd really rather none of the neighbors heard about this. I'm sure I'll be OK."

Dave realized he could probably make no more headway on his own, but was determined to arrange for some protection. He got up, saying, "Have it your way, but I am not going to leave without doing something. Courtney, I really value your friendship, and I realize I am placing it at risk, but you need to know what I am going to do before I leave. I am going over to talk to Anna and ask her to look out for you."

"No! I beg you not to say anything to her." She rose and followed him to the door, tugging at his sleeve.

Dave stopped and turned to face her.

"You do what you have to do. I'll to what I have to do."

Dave opened the door, stopped, and turned back to face her again.

"O.J. Simpson," he said. Then he left.

Anna

After Kate left to attend Mass on her way back to Knoxville, Anna retired to the den to go through an accumulation of unopened mail from the last three days. She sorted through the pile, putting *Time Magazine*, the *Annals of Internal Medicine* and the *Journal of the American Medical Association* off to one side for perusal later in the week. The credit card statements went into one of the baskets labeled *Anna's Safe Place* for immediate attention. There were a few birthday cards, newsletters from church and assorted charities she supported, plus the inevitable requests for donations to political candidates and other organizations she did not support. These went straight into the wastebasket.

As she turned back to the desk, she noticed the gift Roger had brought, still unopened. She removed the wrapping and found a book and a smaller package. The book was one Roger had recently published, with a warm greeting to her on the inside cover. Its title was *What Would Luther Do Today?* Anna recalled that Roger had done a great deal of research on Martin Luther's life. He had even spent a month in Germany a few years ago. Fluent in German, he had likely spent most of his time reading in dusty archives or searching electronic files of old and rare documents. The other package was from Beth. It was a box of German chocolate confections with a short note that said: *This may make the reading more palatable.* Anna had been careful to note in her invitations to the party that no gifts were expected or allowed, but as usual, Beth and Roger marched to their own drummers.

As she was paging through the book to get a sense of Roger's focus, the doorbell rang. Opening the door, she found Dave Brunk standing there with a look of near panic on his face. Feigning surprise, she said, "Oh, hi, Dave, did you leave something behind at the party? Come in."

Dave stepped into the foyer and said, "No, I think I have everything in the car. But if you have a few minutes, I have something important to discuss with you."

"Of course. Come into the living room. Coffee? We have lots of leftovers if you haven't had breakfast yet."

He shook his head. "Thanks. I've already eaten. I need to get back to Dayton before noon today, but Courtney needs help and I hope you can oblige."

Anna took a seat in her favorite recliner, while Dave moved a chair over so he could face her. He quickly outlined the events of the previous evening and the crisis he had found this morning when he went back, ostensibly to pick up some hostas.

Anna was horrified at what she heard, but quickly grasped the gravity of the situation. "My God, she never indicated to me that things were so serious. I knew they had spats from time to time, but she always made light of them. How did you manage to figure this out so fast?"

"I happened to be in the kitchen when Alan called last night. She cut him off very quickly and disconnected the phone so he couldn't call back. At first I thought this was just another lover's tiff but the way she spoke about their relationship tipped me off. She kept blaming herself for provoking the arguments. As a child growing up in an abusive family, I could smell that dynamic right off."

Anna was surprised to hear this. She and her colleagues were aware that Dave came from a very wealthy

New England family. His father in particular had a well-known name in financial circles, and Dave would sometimes deprecatingly refer to some honor bestowed upon him or his mother, who was an honorary chair of many arts organizations. All she could say was, "Oh my . . ."

Dave smiled wryly. "Well, of course you don't display the dirty laundry to the public. People would often ask me why I didn't join the family dynasty and become a financier."

"Why didn't you?"

"Dad expected all three sons to come into the business and work their way up through the ranks to eventually become Vice-President in charge of something useless. I started out to get a degree in business management but found it boring. I took science and physiology courses instead. But I was appalled at his constant demeaning of my mother and me. He was never physically abusive, but he seemed to delight in belittling any achievements we kids made, and making fun of any accolades she received for her volunteer activities."

"You are right on about the psychological abuse. It is different only in kind from physical abuse, but equally destructive. I am astonished you survived with intact self-esteem. When I retired I did some volunteer work at the domestic violence center. It was a revelation to hear how these women were brain-washed into believing they had no thoughts worth expressing, no contributions to make to the family other than the drudge work. Most devastating was the final insult, the belief they had no options. Abusers are very skillful in isolating their partners from friends and family, so that for practical purposes, they might just as well be in a prison."

Dave nodded. "My mother was the affirming parent, along with teachers who made it clear that I was smart, and could choose just about any career I wanted. I never could persuade my mother to break off the relationship. She placed great value on the family reputation and could not imagine doing anything to cast doubt on it. I guess she was willing to pay the price for her lofty status in society."

"So your interest in physiology led you to medicine?"

"Yes. I loved investigative medicine and almost went into pure research, but I also love working directly with patients. But you said you volunteered in a shelter? That's fantastic. Do you think you could help Courtney?" For the first time that morning Dave looked optimistic.

"I still have some contacts at the shelter, and will call to see about the best way to approach a reluctant victim."

"That's great. I am worried that the locks can't get changed until tomorrow. She is willing to do that, but she won't hear of getting a restraining order. Or asking you for a night's shelter. I told her I was going to talk to you anyway, and that really pissed her off."

"Well, that makes it easier for me to get right to the point when I call. Maybe I can start by asking if I can examine her to see if she needs to get Xrays or needs stitches. That kind of turns the attention away from the humiliating aspects of her problem."

"I used that ploy about being a doctor to get my foot in the door this morning."

Dave stood up and wrote something on a slip of paper. "Here's my cell phone number. Please call or text me with any news you have, good or bad. And thanks for being here for her." He embraced Anna warmly and left the house.

Anna leaned back and took a deep breath. She was on the verge of castigating herself for being an actor in this unforeseen drama. *Stop it*, she told herself. That particular drama was already starting its inexorable path the day Courtney and Alan started dating. David just escalated it. If not he, something else would have eventually led to disaster. She debated whether to call or just go over to see if Courtney would talk to her. If she went now, Courtney might still be stubbornly fuming over Dave's remarks, and resent her offer of help. If she waited too long, Alan might appear on the scene and wheedle himself back into her good graces. As she was pondering the merits of the two approaches, she called her contacts at the shelter and got some information about how abused women could apply for asylum, steps they could take for protection, what they should bring with them to the shelter, and what legal steps might need to be taken. It occurred to her that the shelter was always asking for donations of personal care items and clothing. She quickly put together a pillow case full of various items any woman would want during an extended stay, and walked over to Courtney's house.

She rang the doorbell, and after a short while heard Courtney say, "Who is it?"

"It's Anna. I have some supplies you might be able to use." Anna hoped she looked calm and unperturbed.

The door opened. "Come in." Courtney was turned so that the least battered part of her face was toward Anna.

Anna went in and got right to the sore spot. "Dave made it clear that he was instructed not to come and talk to me, but he did. So just tell me what I can do to help. I have cold packs, ace bandages, pain pills, and whatever support you want from me."

Courtney sighed. "I'm so confused. I don't know where to start first. I managed to find the number for a locksmith and found one who is willing to do this on a Sunday. I need to call the agency for temp jobs and tell them I can't work the next few days. I sure hope that doesn't do damage to my record." The two walked back to the kitchen.

"Well, I am willing to stay here until the locks get changed. I agree with Dave, that you are not safe right now."

"I think Dave over-reacted. I know Alan well enough to know that he will calm down and want to apologize and work out our differences. But I don't want him to have a key any more. And much as I like him, I am becoming more and more convinced that we are not a good match."

Anna knew this was not the time to point out that this situation was well beyond the settling of normal 'differences', so she just said, "It might be helpful for you to have an opportunity to talk with other women who have faced the same problems."

Courtney was no dummy and immediately knew where this was going. "Dave said something about a shelter. Did he ask you to persuade me?"

"No, he did not ask me to talk you into a shelter," said Anna, which was technically the truth. She had made the reference to the shelter before he asked for her help. "I mentioned to him that I had volunteered in our local domestic violence center and that I thought it could help. I have some telephone numbers and information about them for you." She handed her a small folder containing the information. Courtney put it on the table.

"Thanks. I'll look at it later."

Anna decided to try another tack. "I also brought over some already chilled cold packs and some bandages. You really need to lie down to help the swelling subside. Let me put the packs where they will do some good. The good news is that the face has such a robust circulation that it heals faster than other areas of the body."

Courtney reluctantly agreed to lie down on the sofa so that Anna could minister to her. After putting the packs in place she said. You need to apply these for about 20 minutes several times a day. Tuesday you can switch to hot packs to speed up the absorption of the bruising. Then with some heavy makeup you can go back to work."

Just then, the door opened. Alan walked in carrying a bouquet of roses. He was a muscular man of medium height and stocky build. Thick dark hair and a short beard framed a square face. He was not particularly handsome, but he had a confident bearing and steady brown eyes giving the impression of a likeable and trustworthy person. Ignoring Anna, he walked over to Courtney, bent over and kissed her on the forehead, murmuring something Anna could not hear. Undecided how she should greet him, she chose to say nothing.

Alan turned to Anna and said, "Courtney and I would like to talk in private."

His manner suggested that he was in charge and would brook no opposition. Anna had seen him from a distance many times but rarely engaged in any significant conversation other than stock pleasantries about the weather or the latest football game. A flood of responses flowed through her mind, most of them likely to escalate the already tense situation. Instead she turned to Courtney and raised an eyebrow, hoping to signal that the ball was in her court.

Somewhere from under layers of hope, resentment, loyalty, despair, and dreams of a future free of distress, a fragment of a younger and braver Courtney emerged.

"Courtney has no interest in a private conversation," she said directly addressing Alan. "Anything you have to say can be said in the presence of my friend." She put heavy emphasis on the last word.

Alan's face flushed. He started to say something, but quickly stopped, apparently concluding that he was outnumbered at the moment. He placed the roses on the kitchen counter and simply said, "I came to tell you how sorry I am. I don't know what came over me last night. What I did was despicable. Please forgive me."

Courtney had heard this before, but this time it sounded false. "You are right. It was despicable. But I am in no shape to talk to you now. Please leave. I will call you in a few days."

Anna thought it was now safe to leave. She opened the door and waved to Courtney saying, mostly to warn Alan, "I'll be back with some lunch in a bit."

Kate

After leaving Mass at Our Lady of Sorrows Catholic Church, and vowing that she had completed a lifetime of penances, which absolved her of any indebtedness to whatever deity she had made promises to, Kate drove home without further incident. As usual, dinner was waiting for her when she arrived. She was greeted warmly by Michael who had two glasses of red wine and some chips and salsa on the living room coffee table.

"Simple fare tonight," said Michael. "Eggplant parmesan, which will be done in about 15 minutes." They retired to the couch to enjoy the wine and trade stories about their adventures at Anna's party.

"You've been home a good two hours ahead of me. What cross have you managed to nail yourself to today?"

He laughed. "Sorry to disappoint you. I have done nothing more exciting than start some laundry and fix dinner for tonight. By the way, there is a letter for you from TennHealth. Might be important."

"Probably my job description, which is still a work in progress. I'll read it tomorrow. I don't want to think about work tonight."

They enjoyed a leisurely dinner and returned to the living room to commune with their respective laptops. Buspar was curled up on an adjoining couch. Michael was busy catching up on various Facebook accounts, intermittently chuckling and occasionally casting aspersions on the sanity of those referenced in other people's posts. Kate relaxed by playing an online version of

Sudoku. By nine she was feeling ready to retire for the evening. The phone rang. It was Anna.

"Well, hey there," Kate said. "I know I forgot to send you a text when I got here. Sorry about that."

"Not a problem. Have you got a minute? Or maybe 30 minutes?"

"I'm afraid to ask why. Let me guess. Roger has decided he likes Harvey Schulman better than Beth and she has had a meltdown. Or Damncat is missing again and you wonder if he is in my trunk."

"Not even close. Remember we saw Dave's car over at Courtney's house?"

"So they now have the hots for each other and are going to run off and live happily until the next divorce?"

"I am not sure about the hots part, but I have just spent the last four hours learning that there is a lot more to Dave than I had ever imagined. It seems that under the trappings of the wealthy playboy dabbling in a medical career for diversion beats the heart of a knight in shining armor."

"That's a good way to get my attention," replied Kate, as she shut down her laptop and closed it. "I take it that Courtney is the damsel in distress."

"Indeed. I never had a clue about what was going on with the boyfriend. She would occasionally say something about a spat and how she was going to swear off men and join a cloister, but she would laugh about it so I didn't pay much attention to those comments. About a week ago she looked like she was down in the dumps. I knew she was having financial stress after she lost her full time job, and asked her how the job hunting was going. She said she had a temp job as a secretary and was managing fairly well on that front, but that she had decided to call it quits with Alan, saying something about not really being compatible as a couple."

"Better to find out now than after marriage, as was my misfortune," Kate said drily.

"Yes, indeed, but apparently Alan was not about to accept that, and began harassing her on a daily basis, I guess thinking he could force a reconciliation."

"That sounds scary. Did he stalk her?"

"No, but he would alternate between wooing her back and angry outbursts when she did not respond. As you might imagine, she was ambivalent because he could be so charming at times."

"Then along comes Dave, who is another charmer."

"Yes. I think she began to make comparisons which confused her even more."

"Is Dave actually interested in developing a relationship?"

"I don't know, and maybe he doesn't either. But what happened was that after the party he walked her back home, and while they were talking Alan called. Courtney. She cut him off abruptly and disconnected the phone. It seems he decided to drive over and saw Dave leaving the house and driving off in his flashy Porsche."

"Please don't tell me someone got killed," said Kate, squeezing her eyes shut in anticipation of horrible news.

Michael looked up anxiously. "Is that Anna? What's wrong?"

Kate held up a hand and mouthed the word *Wait*.

Anna continued. "Not quite that bad, but bad enough. He followed Dave for a few blocks, then came back and beat the shit out of Courtney. Then left her."

For the benefit of Michael, Kate repeated what she had heard. "So nothing happened to Dave, but Courtney got beat up?"

"Yes. Dave had told her he would come back in the morning and pick up some plants she had promised to give him. When he arrived, she wouldn't let him in at first, but apparently he had learned a bit about the conflict with the boyfriend the night before, and figured out that his visit with Courtney had precipitated a crisis. He was very persistent, and she finally let him in. He spent some time tending her wounds and trying to talk her into getting some protection from the police, even suggested a domestic violence shelter."

"Not bad for a nephrologist to figure that out."

"That's the other interesting part. It seems his own father was a psychological abuser while posing as the local pillar of integrity and virtue in his professional and social lives. Dave is very familiar with the dynamics of domestic abuse, and even though he knows it takes a long time for a woman to grasp the reality of her situation, he was pretty persistent. After he left her house, he came over to mine and asked me to do what I could to help."

"You volunteered in a women's shelter a few years ago, didn't you?"

"Yes. I was able to put together some information, and went over with that and ice packs and bandages to see what I could accomplish."

"Any luck?"

"She was reluctant at first to let me in, but she did, and I was glad to hear that she was about to have the locks changed, but she has no interest in getting a restraining order or calling the shelter."

"Do you think she can break off with Alan?"

"Interesting question. He came over with a bouquet while I was there. Made it clear that I should leave since they needed a private conversation."

"Good grief! What did you do?"

"I just sat there. Decided that if anyone was going to throw me out, it had to be Courtney."

"And . . ."

"Courtney suddenly summoned up some dormant assertiveness and told him that if he had anything to say, it would be in the presence of her friend."

"And I wasn't there to see this drama. I am so envious!"

Anna laughed. "He turned a bit red at that point and was obviously working hard at being civil and non-threatening. When Courtney said politely that she thought it best that he leave, he must have decided that he had lost this round. So he tried to resurrect some dignity with expressions of affection and concern."

"So where do things stand now?"

"I called Dave to give him an update. He was somewhat relieved, but does not think she is out of danger. He said that when abusers find themselves losing control, regaining it becomes a central driver of their behavior, even if it is self-destructive. His parting words to her were about OJ Simpson."

"You are right about the shining armor. I had no idea about Dave's family background, or that he would be willing to intervene at this level."

"I saw her after the locksmith arrived, and told her I thought she should spend the night with me. She is reluctant to do that, so I plan stay up as late as I can and watch for the black SUV."

Kate had put the last part of the conversation on speakerphone so Michael could hear. After bidding Anna good night, Kate hung up and looked at him.

"Ready to write those memoirs yet?" he asked with a wry smile.

Finale

Anna barely slept Sunday night, awakening to a gray cloudy sky, which matched her mood. She had persuaded Courtney to put her cell phone under her pillow and call 911 if she heard anything suspicious in or around the house. The locks had been changed, so that was one small comfort to both of them. She called Courtney and was relieved to hear that there had been no contact from Alan during the night. However, she had no plans other than to lie low for a few days and go back to work on Wednesday.

"Let me know if you need anything. I can bring lunch or dinner over if you want," said Anna.

"Thanks. I'm good for right now on the food."

Anna immediately called Dave to give him an update. He thanked her profusely, obviously relieved.

"I want to come back to talk to her this week," he said. "I think I may be able to help her out of the quagmire."

"Short of dispatching Alan yourself, what do you think is possible?"

"I have a lot of connections in the financial community and have started some conversations with people who might be interested in becoming investors in the Bed and Breakfast she wants to start. I want to know if she is prepared to relocate in another city, which would place some distance between her and Alan."

"Perchance is Dayton the other city?" asked Anna mischievously.

"Not necessarily. Dayton is not doing well economically. It's best to look for a market that gets a lot of tourists and doesn't have a glut of B & B's. She needs some expert help in that direction, and I can provide that."

Anna was again astounded at Dave's commitment to help and at his skill in analyzing the options. "Dave, I didn't get a chance to say this yesterday, but I want you to know that you are an amazing person. I'm proud to call you my friend. Just call Courtney now and tell her what you told me. I am sure she will welcome another meeting with you."

"OK. Stay in touch."

Anna hung up the phone, leaned back and sighed. She reflected on the tumultuous events of the last few days. *And what is already written in the next chapter of our lives? Will Beth and Roger decide to live together? Or remarry? Can Pat and Ted survive as a devoted couple, or will one of them decide it's time to marry someone else? Will Dave and Courtney find a relationship beyond business? Can Kate survive another adventure? What will my next adventure be?* She started to sing a favorite old Quaker hymn.

> My life flows on in endless song;
> Above earth's lamentation,
> I hear the sweet, tho' far-off hymn
> That hails a new creation;
> Thro' all the tumult and the strife
> I hear the music ringing;
> It finds an echo in my soul—
> How can I keep from singing?

About the Author

Alice Faryna was born on a small farm operated by her parents, both immigrants from Poland and grateful for the opportunity to give their four children the college education never available to them. They supported her desire to go beyond undergraduate school. She was among three women admitted to the University of Rochester School of Medicine and Dentistry in 1953. During a career that spanned 40 years, she worked in a variety of settings all over the United States: private practice, neighborhood health centers, VA hospitals, research in paramedical professions, and academic medicine at Wright State University. Her final career was an administrative job in the Medicare program. All these experiences inspired her to write a novel illuminating the daily lives of a group of medical colleagues grappling with personal problems while working within a system undergoing disturbing changes affecting their professional lives and the lives of their patients.

www.ingramcontent.com/pod-product-compliance
Lightning Source LLC
Chambersburg PA
CBHW070846120626
46556CB00002B/902